FORBIDDEN PLUNDER

BY JESSICA KILLABREW

This Work is fiction. All organizations, events, and characters named or referenced in this work are products of the author's imagination or used fictitiously.

ISBN-10# 1-945012-38-2
ISBN-13# 978-1-945012-38-9

Edited by Vinvatar Publishing

Artwork by Vinvatar Publishing

Published by Vinvatar Publishing
Website: Vinvatar.com

TABLE OF CONTENTS

PART 1

A PIRATE'S LIFE

CHAPTER 1

Alexander patiently waited as his father walked toward him with another woman on his arm. He knew what it was about, as always. The woman wasn't as bad looking as the last one, she was actually beautiful. She had dark waves of hair that hung over her elegant green dress. Her smile was as beautiful as most of the woman he had seen. However, he still felt no attraction to her.

"I will leave you two alone for a second while I go fetch Mrs. Boseuilla." His Father said as soon as he and the lady reached him.

"Good Evening, Milady. What might I have the pleasure of calling you by?" Alex said as soon as his father turned to leave.

"Ava." The lady said as her mocha colored cheeks turned a light shade of red. She put her hand out towards Alexander.

"Alexander." He answered as he lifted her hand to his lips and lightly placed a kiss on the knuckles.

"So you are Mr. Boseuilla's son? He has been talking about you to just about every woman I know."

"Yes." He answered.

They barely got a chance to speak before his father came out and handed Ava a ring. "Now Miss Ava I would be proud if you were to marry my son, say at the end of the week?" His father said.

"I would be glad to." Ava answered.

"Are you insane Father?" Alexander argued. "You have barely even given us a chance to speak, and you are already proposing for me." His voice was loud and filled with the anger he felt.

"Alexander." His father started. "How could you be so rude; in front of the woman you are supposed to wed?"

"I am not marrying someone you choose for me." He yelled. He turned to Ava. "No offense meant towards you Ava." He added.

"I've given you time to choose for yourself, now it is my turn, you two will wed at the end of the week, or I will have the authorities after you for whatever I can, maybe I'll even throw you onto a Naval ship." His father returned.

"You can go ahead and do whatever you want father, but I am not marrying someone I just met."

"Her family is just as wealthy as ours."

"Dammit, I will never marry for wealth, you might as well call the authorities now." He said then stormed up the stairs to his room, cursing his father for being a pompous arse like the rest of the wealthy he knew. He hated the way his family was, and the way they treated the other people, as if they were just objects and the only thing that mattered was the money they were worth. It was despicable.

Alexander stood in the veranda doorway, pondering the day's events. His family had some strange idea of him marrying a woman strictly for wealth, he wished his father wasn't as worried about wealth as he was. He couldn't complain much, she was beautiful, about his age, and at least, her wealth was just as good as his, but he wanted more, he knew there was something more than what his parents had, he had seen it a few times, more often between the servants that worked around their house than any of the people his family associated with. He felt absolutely no connection to the women that his father had chosen for him, but his parents didn't care.

Alex was the kind of man who didn't care about money, he would rather marry some servant girl than marry just for money. He wanted to find more than what his parents wanted for him, however they had put their foot down today.

He was being forced to wed the woman by the end of the week, and he wasn't sure what would happen if he didn't, his father would probably turn him into the authorities for adultery or something like that. He packed a bag, full of his clothes, and was glad he chose not to dress like all the other pompous rich bastards in that town. He grabbed the money he had earned from working his father's tobacco business when they went out of town, and he jumped down from his veranda, disappearing into the night as quickly and quietly as possible.

He got to the end of the town and bought a horse from a stableman, then continued, heading toward the nearest harbor. He had to get as far away as possible, he couldn't live like his mother and father. He knew they never really loved each other and also knew that they fought more often than not, since he was a child. They were miserable, even behind their fake smiles it was obvious.

His hatred for his father grew stronger and stronger every time he heard the horses hooves bang against the ground. He was glad that his father often took him to Veracruz to trade tobacco once in a while, or he was sure he would have never found his way there.

When he showed up at Veracruz, there was only one place that was still open, and it was known for the pirate's that often showed up. It was always loud and rowdy, his father had stopped in a few times for a drink. Alex wished he could have made it to Veracruz a little earlier so he could find a nicer place to rest but there was no such luck for him tonight.

He found himself a table close to the bar and wasn't all that surprised when a man walked over to him. Alex had watched the way everyone was addressing the man as Captain, so he knew if he were to be nice to anyone in that place it should be him. As he plopped down in the chair next to him Alex smiled.

“Let me buy you a drink sir.” Alex said waiving over a bar wench.

“So what be yer story lad, nobody sits here in this bar without a story.” He asked.

“It’s simple, I left home, I couldn’t believe the home life I was having and am looking to change it.” Alex answered.

“Ye look like yer trying to leave?” he asked, his words slurred and sloppy. “Are you running from something?”

“Aye, I am trying to leave, but I’m not running from nothing.” Alex answered, making note of the expensive coat and hat the man was wearing.

“I am transporting some tobacco products to Trinidad in the morning, if yer willing to put in the work, I’m in search of another person for this journey.” The man answered.

“What is the arrangement?” Alex returned.

“You’ll be paid, and if you want to return back to Veracruz we will gladly bring you back since all we do is run back and forth between Trinidad and here.” He answered.

“I won’t be returning but I’ll go with you over there.” Alex returned.

“That’s too bad, we could use another merchant, but I can tell yer looking for bigger things. The name is Bartholomew.”

“Alex.” He returned not wanting to give his full name, he knew the merchant was probably one of his father’s and he’d be caught fairly quickly.

"Let's get you aboard me ship then." Bartholomew said then laid down some coin for the drinks on the table.

Alex grabbed his bag, thinking that was too easy for him. He thought he was going to have to work to find a way out of Veracruz before his Father, Alejandro Boseuilla, would get to Veracruz to get pay for the merchandise as he called it.

Alex got put in a bunkroom with five other people, he was thankful that he found a place to rest his head for the night, he hadn't realized how tired he was until then. He tossed his duffel onto the foot of the bunk and climbed up. He was able to fall asleep as soon as his head hit the pillow.

Alexander woke to shouting and banging on the door. He jumped out of bed along with all the other men in the room. He ran up onto the deck of the ship and had no clue what he was doing. He went and found someone that looked like they needed help and joined in as they started lifting the anchor, turning the capstan as far as it would go to the right. Once the anchor was up they had to start climbing the masts and dropping the sails. Alex had no clue that there would be that much work first thing in the morning on the ship, but he was sure that there was more to come.

Bartholomew walked over to him then. "Since ye are the new person aboard the ship, ye will get to swab my deck." He said as he handed Alex a mop and a bucket.

He didn't want to protest it, but he didn't like the idea of it, so he just took to mop and bucket and started mopping up the wooden ship, that honestly didn't even look to be dirty. He had no clue what he had gotten himself into but it had to better than what his father was putting him through. As he sat there mopping the deck of the ship, he thought about how his life was with his mother and father when he was younger.

He remembered the cold looks they would give each other. There was no love in the expressions they would share. Neither of the two bothered to spend any time with him, usually leaving him with a nanny, her name was Griselda but she was no better to attend to him than his parents were. He grew close to a servant named Hillary when Griselda would let him run free. His father only started paying attention to him when he was old enough to learn how to take care of the company when he was gone, and even then he was bitter and cold. He started to dislike his father more and more every time they spent any time together. It got even worse when he was old enough to marry and up till he left. He couldn't have made a better decision than this.

The sun beat down on his back as he continued his work, until the entire ship was clean, from the quarter deck all the way down to the brig, which was at the bottom of the boat, he wasn't sure why they needed cells on a merchant ship but he cleaned them anyway.

He was exhausted by the time he was finished, and completely famished. He was glad when he finished and food was handed to him, however it was not like anything he had ever eaten before.

It looked like porridge or oatmeal, but tasted foul, but he was too hungry to care. Finishing his food as quickly as possible so he didn't have to taste it all that much, he went to bed as soon as he noticed the rest of the men were going to bed. He was so drained from the first day he was surprised he was able to do all the stuff and keep up. However, it wasn't as easy for him to fall asleep that night. He had a sense of adventure going for him, especially now that he had stepped out of the boundaries that his parent's had set up for him. He laid there for a while, ready for the next day to come as he thought about how different his life had become over just one day.

*****

Alex was almost surprised at how quickly everything was going. He had lost track of time, his muscles were aching and his entire body was sore, but they were to reach Trinidad first thing in the morning. Then he would have nothing left to do with his father. He would find a way to get further away, he would no longer be Alexander, just Alex and as far as he was concerned no one would need to know of his last name. He couldn't wait to start his new life, and decided he would stick to the life of sailing.

The constant smell of the ocean and the feel of the waves rolling underneath his feet were a new found comfort, he was even starting to get used to the foul tasting gruel they were fed on a daily basis. He couldn't imagine surrendering to land again. The sea would be his new life, his new love.

This day went by as quickly as the rest until they heard it. "Enemy flags approaching, they've raised their blacks Captain." The announcement thundered loudly even though the man announcing it was at the top of the crow's nest.

"All hands on deck, we go down fighting." Captain Bartholomew yelled.

Of course this had to happen now. Now he was going to die by a pirate's hand, just his luck. Things had to be going right for once and of course something happened. Shit, he didn't have a gun or a sword. He readied himself the best he could. He would have to knock down the easiest prey and steal their sword or gun, whatever they had. He wondered if he could even do it though, he had been in his fair share of fist fights but never anything with a weapon, he used to pretend to sword fight as a child but he had no clue if it was anything like it would be.

The ship crashed into the side of the ship he was on almost knocking him over. He caught his footing just to see a group of people swinging over on ropes. He saw a scrawny older man start swing over and ran to where he was sure he would land on the deck. As soon as he landed he drilled his fist at the man's face, putting all his weight into that one swing, he didn't give him a chance to catch his footing beforehand. The man fell over then and Alex stomped on his wrist forcing his hand off the blade he held.

Taking the sword, Alex thought about the times he and Hilary would sword fight, when he was a child, of course it was with nothing more than the sticks that they had found on the ground. He had never killed a man before either. The one he had just hit was now unconscious on the deck, his heart was pounding so loudly in his head it was giving him a headache. Then he heard hurried footsteps running up behind him he turned and held the sword up, barely blocking the other man's swing. He quickly countered with his own swing and kicked his foot out at the same time knocking the man overboard. Shit he just killed a man.

As the adrenaline surged through his body he realized he wasn't fighting to win, he was fighting to survive and it was exhilarating. He quickly moved around the fallen men on the deck, and swung his sword at the next standing person he saw, but he hadn't realized that he just took on the Pirate Captain. Barely blocking swing after swing he quickly lost his footing and before he knew it he was staring up the shiny blade to a heavily ringed hand.

"Ye sure be a fighter lad." He said. "One I could definitely use aboard me ship. I need some men with yer will to live."

"What's in it for me?" Alex asked, swallowing the non-existent lump in his throat that seemed to grow every time the blade came closer to his throat.

"I'll let ye live." He answered.

Alex glanced around the ship to see that most the other merchant men were tied up or dead. Bartholomew was standing with his arms over his head as a few of the pirates took off everything but his breeches. "I'm in." Alex answered.

He put out his hand and pulled Alex to his feet. "Welcome aboard the red diamond." He said. "I be Captain Billy and that is all ye shall ever need to know about me. Load the plunder and get yer arses back over the gangway before I leave ye with the merchant ship, we need to get to Tortuga quick for the repairs to the ship, and I wouldn't mind getting me some coin while we be there." He yelled. "Ye lad, need to come with me and read through the articles of agreement, and sign 'em."

Alex still felt his adrenaline rushing, it was almost so bad he could feel the blood coursing through his veins, however he went to grab his duffle and then followed Captain Billy aboard the ship. Captain Billy pointed to the mast behind the rest of them, "the articles be up on the mizzenmast lad, go read and agree."

He walked over to the mast, or the mizzenmast as Captain Billy called it and began to read over the parchment paper that was posted to it.

Articles Of Agreement

I. Every Man Shall obey civil Command; the Captain shall have one full Share and a half of all Prizes; the Master, Carpenter, Boatswain and Gunner shall have one Share and quarter. All other men shall receive one share.

II. If any Man shall offer to run away, or keep any Secret from the Company, he shall be marooned with one Bottle of Powder, one Bottle of Water, one small Arm, and one Shot.

III. If any Man shall steal any Thing in the Company, or game, to the Value of a Piece of Eight, he shall be marooned or shot by the company offended.

IV. If any time we shall meet another Marooner that Man shall sign his Articles without the Consent of our Company, shall suffer such Punishment as the Captain and Company shall think fit.

V. That Man that shall strike another whilst these Articles are in force, shall receive Moses' Law (that is, 40 lashes lacking one) on the bare Back.

VI. That Man that shall snap his Arms, or smoke Tobacco in the Hold, without a Cap to his Pipe, or carry a Candle lit without a

Lanthorn, shall suffer the same Punishment as in the former Article.

VII. No Women aboard the ship, if a woman found stowaway she shall be marooned with one Bottle of Powder, one Bottle of Water, one small Arm, and one Shot.

It was a simple decision for Alex, he was going to sign, considering that the captain already said he would kill him if he didn't, plus he didn't want to stay aboard that merchant ship forever, he would probably end up here eventually. He looked at all the other signatures, only first names on most, some had initials instead of first names, and other's had last names also. He just simply signed Alex and walked back over to where the captain was. Billy showed him down to where he would be sleeping and he wasn't shocked to see that it was set up the same, a lot of the Spanish Galleons were the only difference was usually in size, this one was thankfully bigger.

He looked over all the bunks, not many of them were taken, only two others and the one he was taking, but there was enough bunks for a total of six, and plenty room to add more. He tossed his bag on the bed. Billy looked at him then and raised an eyebrow.

"I do believe ol' Oliver will be wantin' his sword back if'n ye want any pay." Captain Billy said. "As long as ye didn't kill 'im that is."

"No, he's alive, I needed it then; he can have it back now." Alex answered.

"Ye mean to tell me that ye took Oliver's sword unarmed?" Billy asked, even more shocked than he was before.

"Yes, I needed it at the time, and I found one that I could get." Alex repeated.

"I be sure glad to have ye aboard me ship lad, never heard of that one happenin' before." He laughed as he spoke.

Alex handed Billy the sword and they started walking back up to the deck, he was still laughing and was barely able to hold his cool when Oliver walked up to him. "Ye got me sword back Captain how kind of ye." Oliver said, trying not to seem too irritated.

"Sorry bout that." Alex said as he scratched his head.

"Listen up crew, this here be Alex, and he is new so show him how things go around here, considering he could take another man's sword unarmed I can assure ye all he will be a great addition." He announced. "Now Oliver be the quartermaster, he's in charge of the splitting the pay among the crew, Henry over there be the Navigator, he makes the ship go wherever I tell him to, Richard is the Bosun, he will be telling ye what needs to be done. Clarence is the master gunner, he takes care of the gun and shot and has them ready when there be a battle coming, Isaac is the Master Carpenter, he will oversee and assist with all repairs to the ship, but he does most of them. Adam repairs the sails, and makes them when need, he's called the sail maker but we all like to call him a seamstress. Then you have Hugh, he's the cook, Philip is the surgeon. Then the other sailors George, John, Martin, and James."

Alex was barely able to keep up with the faces and names but he knew he would catch on with time, and hopefully make a few friends. He nodded his head at them all, just before the captain yelled again. "Get me damn ship headed to Tortuga damn it." They all jumped to get the ship headed in the right direction. This was definitely going to be a change of pace for him.

The crew all got the ship turned around and they all headed to bed as soon as they were clear of the Merchant ship. Once again the excitement kept Alex tossing and turning, fighting for his sleep. He knew this could either be a turn for the worst or a turn for the best, but now that he signed aboard a pirate ship, he could never go home, and that was exactly what he wanted.

CHAPTER 2

Christina fumbled as she started pouring the glass of rum for her master. She heard him yell and almost dropped the glass, she quickly recovered from the shock. He was already on his fourth glass and she knew his temper was getting bad. She quickly carried the glass into him. "Here sir." She answered.

His normal grey eyes looked bloodshot. His dark hair was messy. He was a big guy, not necessarily fat, just stout. He looked fearsome and had a deep booming voice most the time.

He yanked the glass out of her hand. She was startled by the gruffness in his voice as he lashed out at her. "What took you so long?" It wasn't even a question and she knew it, it was a demand for her to be faster next time.

"I'm sorry Sir, it won't happen next time." She answered.

He downed the glass quicker than she thought possible. Before she had a chance to walk away he grabbed her by her arm and pulled her down to the couch. Before she had a chance to say anything he took her lips in a rough kiss. She wriggled in a panic underneath him as she fought to get herself free.

"Excuse me sir but that is inappropriate behavior." She said when she finally got herself free. She had been warned by the other servants about this, but she wasn't going to let herself be another one of his victims.

"You are my servant and you will do whatever I want you to." His voice cracked down like thunder booming through house.

He started to pull up her dress, she began to panic, her heart practically jumping into her throat as the fear coursed through her veins. She was scared, frozen in terror. She snapped out of it quickly and struggled to push him off of her. She started to swing at him, hoping she could get in one good hit, but with all of his body weight on top of her it was to no avail. He grabbed her arms then and held her down, ripping her dress open with little effort. Whilst he tried to unbuckle his belt she got one arm free and reached for the nearest thing and slammed it against his head. Shit, she just broke his lamp. His body fell limp on top of her and blood started dripping down his head.

She pushed him off of her. She checked for a pulse, but couldn't find it. She just killed a man, a noble man at that. He had breakfast plans the next morning too, he was planning on meeting with the mayor over using one of his boats, she had to leave now.

Feeling sick to her stomach, she lost all of the food she had eaten for the last few days as her guts spilled out on the floor. The horrendous sight of a dead man laying on the floor had her nauseated. Her heart started to race and she could feel her body getting ready to vomit once again. She quickly covered the body with a sheet.

Knowing she would get caught if she stayed in the same clothes because of the blood she ran up to his room and sewed the waistband of a pair of breeches to fit her. She used a fabric to flatten her chest down and tied her hair back. She added one of his smaller shirts to the outfit and found one of his beautiful tricornered hats. She put it on and dirtied her face enough to look like a young boy. She disappeared into the night, going straight to the harbor. In a panic she was willing to hop on the first boat willing to take her away.

Hearing a rowdy bunch of Pirate's talking about needing extra people as they tripped over each other, she deepened her voice as much as possible. Scared beyond all relief, her heart trying to jump out of her chest. "I'll be your cabin boy." She said, having to choke the words out as she tried to hide her shaky hands.

The lot of them started laughing at her. "Lad ye look to be fifteen years old." One of them said through the booming drunken laughter.

"What's it matter to you? You're all pirates aren't ye?" She returned trying not to act like a woman would in this sort of situation.

"The boy has a point, Alex take him aboard the ship and 'ave him sign the articles of agreement.

"Yes captain." Alex said as he stepped out from behind the captain.

Christina's heart stopped as she saw him standing there. His body raging with muscles like she had never seen. His long dark hair was tied back, his dark brown eyes mystifying as all hell. His moustache and goatee accentuated his face just right. Bloody hell how was she supposed to act like a man with such a man aboard the ship. Her knees were already weak at the sight of his golden tan skin, let alone the features that came with it.

Alex led her up the gangway and onto the deck of the ship. Her stomach was turning like never before. He led her over to the last mast on the ship. "Read the articles before you sign, lad." He said.

Articles Of Agreement

I. Every Man Shall obey civil Command; the Captain shall have one full Share and a half of all Prizes; the Master, Carpenter, Boatswain and Gunner shall have one Share and quarter. All other men shall receive one share.

II. If any Man shall offer to run away, or keep any Secret from the Company, he shall be marooned with one Bottle of Powder, one Bottle of Water, one small Arm, and one Shot.

III. If any Man shall steal any Thing in the Company, or game, to the Value of a Piece of Eight, he shall be marooned or shot by the company offended.

IV. If any time we shall meet another Marooner that Man shall sign his Articles without the Consent of our Company, shall suffer such Punishment as the Captain and Company shall think fit.

V. That Man that shall strike another whilst these Articles are in force, shall receive Moses' Law (that is, 40 lashes lacking one) on the bare Back.

VI. That Man that shall snap his Arms, or smoke Tobacco in the Hold, without a Cap to his Pipe, or carry a Candle lit without a Lanthorn, shall suffer the same Punishment as in the former Article.

VII. No Women aboard the ship, if a woman found stowaway she shall be marooned with one Bottle of Powder, one Bottle of Water, one small Arm, and one Shot.

.

She hadn't even thought of a man's name yet. Right there at the bottom it read no women on aboard. Knowing that Alex was waiting for her to sign the Articles she quickly signed Christopher at the bottom. She let out a deep breath.

"Ah, Christopher be yer name lad, tell me how is it that ye seem so eager to board a ship that ye don't seem to care who ye be leaving' with?" He asked.

She looked up into his eyes, losing track of what he had asked, then remembering what happened she realized that she hadn't even thought of an excuse. "I was a servant, and don't want to be anymore." She answered quickly.

"Can't say I blame ye there lad, 'ow old are you really?" He asked.

"Twenty one." She answered.

"I would have taken you for a fifteen year old boy, ye have no facial hair and ye still look a little girly lad." Alex returned.

"I get me looks from me ma." Christina answered.

"Is this yer first time aboard a ship?" He asked.

"Umm, no, I came to Barbados on a ship when I was a lot younger, but I was just a babe, and don't remember anything about it. I came over with my ma after my father died." She answered.

"Alright, well I will be showin' ye the ropes then first thing in the morn, trust me, it's a lot more work than it looks ta be." He stated. "You'll bunk in the empty room with me, it'll be empty till we get to Tortuga and with any luck it will be filled, we have to pick up some of our men that were injured last time we fought."

"What's Tortuga?" Christina asked.

"It's basically an island for us pirates, there be merchants that are willing to buy from our lots, and taverns that be pirate friendly, ah yes, Tortuga be a great place." Alex answered. "Not to mention the wenches that be willing to bed with the likes of us, and the mountains of rum that we could drink till we be sick."

"How long have ye been a sailor?" Christina asked, trying to hide the reddening in her cheeks at the idea of being surrounded by prostitutes.

"It's been about a year, I started out as a cabin boy, like ye, but so far they have come up with a new title for me aboard this ship, Master Swordsman. It's a fake title, but it's better than no title." Alex started.

"How did that happen?" Christina asked, mesmerized by his fascinating story, and sultry voice.

"Well, Captain Billy only brought me on because I was the only one still standing after they overtook the merchant ship I was on. He laughed because I was able to take down one of his men and steal his sword while I was unarmed." He laughed at the memories as he spoke. "Ever since then I guess I became one of the best fighters that he had ever seen, especially with a sword."

"I guess that explains the title." Christina answered, fighting herself to sound like a man.

She followed Alex as he led her down to the bunkroom he was sleeping in. She tossed the bag she had packed onto the foot of the bed, just as his was. She got into the bed trying to move as much like a man as possible.

"Ye don't have much now, do ye lad?" Alex asked.

"I don't need much." Christina returned. She was trying not to think about all the clothes and stuff she had left behind in that monster's house, however she could never go back now, it was all lost to her along with the former her, Christina. She had to leave that person behind. She was now Christopher, a man, with a secret that could never be told to anyone.

She closed her eyes, trying to forget about her former self, trying to forget about her Master's advances on her, trying to forget about her horrible act of murder. She needed to clear her conscious but the only thing she was thinking was that he had tried to hurt her. He would have taken her even though she protested it. As she laid there she could see his life leave his body as she hit him over the head with the lamp. She could feel a tear roll down her cheek, she rolled over so there was no chance that Alex would see.

When she awoke, she was glad she had snapped out of the dream she was having before she could start screaming, she knew what had happened would haunt her she just hoped it wouldn't affect her hiding. She walked out on deck seeing that Alex was already out of the room she figured that was where he was.

He stood up at the top of the deck, she was almost surprised to see him up there alone. "Is there something wrong?" She asked.

"You tell me?" He returned.

"What do you mean?" She asked, thinking she might have said something in her sleep to give her true gender away.

"You kept saying get him off me." Alex stated. "I assume your master beat you."

"Yes, since I was a little g... boy." Christina answered barely able to catch her mistake before it got out.

"Well I have to go get my crew seeing as how they are not here. Would ye like to come with?" He asked.

"No, I'll wait." She answered. She knew with the light being up that someone might be able to recognize her, she also knew that her master would have been found by then.

Alex shrugged it off quickly and left the ship. Then she could hear the bells sounding around town. Shit they must of found him. Before she knew it the pirates were all running out of the tavern to the ship, barely sneaking past the town guards. She giggled at the sight of them all running, most of them were stumbling which wasn't much of a surprise after the way she saw them all last night.

It wasn't long until they all got to the ship. She stopped her girlish laughing and stood straight and tall, trying to seem more like a man than she did yesterday. Yes this was definitely going to be hard for her to do but she would manage, she had too. As soon as they boarded the ship, Alex started to introduce her to everyone as Christopher.

Alex walked over to her when he finished telling everyone of her. "Oliver be the quartermaster, he's in charge of splitting the pay among the crew, Henry over there be the Navigator, and he makes the ship go wherever he is told to, Richard is the Bosun, and he will be telling ye what needs to be done. Clarence is the master gunner, he takes care of the gun and shot and has them ready for when enemy flags are raised, Isaac is the Master Carpenter, he will oversee and assist with all repairs to the ship, but he does most of them. Adam repairs the sails, and makes them when needed, he's called the sail maker but we all like to call him a seamstress. Then you have Hugh, he's the cook, Philip is the surgeon. Then the other sailors George, John, Martin, and James, which George John and Martin are waiting in Tortuga for us to get there." He pointed a finger at all the sailors present.

She felt she had gotten the names with the faces fairly good but knew that she would get a few mixed up. She kept saying the names over and over again in her head trying to picture who Alex pointed at.

She followed Alex as he started pushing on the capstan. She waited for him to tell her to start mopping the deck before she started. When she was done swabbing the deck as they called it, he handed her some tar, and got down to help her, showing her how to do it properly.

"So 'ow bad was he to ye?" He asked as they worked in the blistering sun, conversation was the best way to keep their mind off the heat.

"He was pretty bad, He would slap me for no reason, or if I took too long getting whatever he wanted." She said, trying not to let slip that he had tried to rape her, or that she had killed him.

"That's horrible, I can't blame ye for leaving mate." Alex returned.

"Why did you leave home?" Christina asked.

"The usual, just didn't want to be in Port Royal anymore. My life was too dull and I wanted adventure, so I joined a merchant ship, this nasty band of scallywags picked me up just off the coast of Trinidad." She could tell he was lying.

"I would have taken you for Spanish, not English, because of your accent." She didn't mean for the words to come out so abruptly and stammered to fix it.

"That's actually not the first time I've heard that." He answered, chuckling. "I know I look Spanish, I hear that more often than anything else."

She had to look away from his charming smile before she gave herself away. He had to have the most appealing smile she had ever seen. She needed to get off this ship, before they caught on to her, and that man was going to be the first to make it obvious. He had her stomach tossing and turning every way possible. It was definitely going to be a challenge to keep her identity hidden, this man had her urges completely out of control and there was no way she could come back from it all.

She tried not looking at him as they kept tarring the wooden planks, however she kept stealing glances at his sculpted torso and gorgeous face. She was glad when the crew headed to bed for the night, she didn't hesitate to join them. She laid in her bed and pretended to be asleep as Alex walked in the room.

She wished she could tell him, she would let him do numerous things to her, and the way she kept seeing him naked every time she closed her eyes made her get a tingling in her lower stomach. She had quite the urge for him. She could picture herself under him, and on top of him, where ever he wanted her to be, doing whatever he wanted her to do.

Christina had never had urges that strong for someone, nor had she ever felt a pull that strong, it was even stronger than her need to get away from Barbados. However, she fought herself to believe that nothing could ever come of those urges and that she could never act on them. She forced herself to sleep, pushing the enticing thoughts out of her mind.

CHAPTER 3

Alex knew something was up with the boy that offered to board the ship from the second he addressed him. He looked in a panic and way too eager to leave, he also caught his cheeks bright red when Alex stepped forward to take him to sign the articles. He claimed to be twenty one but Alex thought he looked, and acted younger, like a fifteen year old boy, maybe even a young woman. He also walked like a woman once in a while, and he would catch him stealing glances at him.

Over the few weeks it took for them to get to Tortuga Alex had spent more time with Chris than he did the rest of the crew. He taught the boy how to do almost everything on the ship, including some of what Philip had taught him about surgery, telling him stuff about himself that no one else knew aboard the ship. The connection between the two was almost instant. Christopher was catching on quick and almost as good as the rest of them by the time they hit Tortuga however Alex still had his suspicions about the boy. He had a plan to get him to open up a little more, he was going to get him drunk, so drunk he wouldn't remember what was said.

Honestly Alex had feelings towards the young boy, feelings he would never admit to because of their genders. He found himself stealing glances just as often as he caught Chris doing it too. Catching himself flirting with Chris plenty of times he found himself growing afraid of the reactions he was having towards him. He tried to hide it the best he could for he knew he would get thrown off the ship for it, but he just couldn't get the feeling of closeness to him go away. He also felt very protective, standing up for Chris whenever someone would say something offensive. He honestly doubted that Chris were a man though.

Chris kept all of his clothes on at night, including his hat. He spoke in his sleep, his voice was either not matured or it was a woman's voice. He thought about asking, but didn't want to offend him if he was wrong. He would wait until they made port.

He and Chris started to drop the anchor, not far from shore. Once that was done they all started to get in the longboats and row to the harbor. Alex looked at Chris and noticed that he seemed worried about something. He was definitely hiding something, he had known that since the beginning. Alex knew there was no way he would open up to him sober though so he waited patiently.

Alex walked with Chris to the tavern and sat down at a table close to the bar. He ordered a couple mugs of ale and slid one across the table to Christopher. Before long one of the bar wenches came over and slid herself onto Christopher's lap.

"Well I haven't seen you around here." She said as she played with Christopher's hat.

Christopher's cheeks flushed red and he took a swig of his ale. "Yes I am new here." He didn't even bother to look at the wenches breasts that were in his face at that point.

The wench started rubbing her hands all over Christopher as she whispered sweet nothings in his ear. As soon as she started to move down towards his breeches Christopher grabbed her hand. "Ye won't be finding what yer looking for down there. I don't have the money ye want, and I'd rather have a woman that comes free rather than one that comes with a price and open to any man willing to pay."

The wench stood up quickly and slapped Christopher as hard as she possibly could before she stormed off. Alex couldn't help but laugh. Then one of the bar wenches caught his eye as she made her way towards him.

"Alex, I knew you would be back for me." She said as she made her way onto his lap.

"Ah Samantha, ye be a sight for sore eyes to a lonely old sailor like me." He answered as he rubbed his hand on her arse.

Christina watched as he squeezed the woman's arse but tried to hide the jealousy she was feeling. She wanted to feel his hands all over her, and his lips trailing the flesh on her neck, as he was now doing with the wench. Watching as he took the wenches lips in a deep kiss, she wanted to feel him suck on her lip like that. She felt envious of the wench, and a longing to be the woman she was.

"Shall ye be the one to accompany me to bed tonight?" She whispered in his ear, her bright red lips mere centimeters away from his ear.

"Not tonight my dear, but we will see if tomorrow holds that in the stars for us. How about another round of ales over here." Alex returned.

Christina felt relief as he turned the wench down, but she knew it wasn't for her. It would never be for her, especially with the way she had to dress and act.

The wench lightly stroked the outside of his breeches. "Anything you want." She answered then stood up slowly, letting him get a lingering look at her breasts that were about ready to pop out of her corset.

"Ye better get used to what you can get around here Chris, not many women will sleep with the likes of us." Alex stated.

Chris's cheeks grew red, but he didn't say anything else to him. "I was like that too when I first came here, but it does get lonely being around nothing but pirates." He continued.

"I'm used to being lonely." Christopher answered as he downed the ale that the wench just set down in front of him.

"Ye've never bedded anyone before?" Alex returned.

"That's not it at all." Chris answered.

“It be getting late, we should go find a room for the night, afore it gets too late.” Alex said, downing his ale.

Chris stood up and headed out the door, just a head of Alex. The streets were busy, filled with pirates. As soon as Alex walked out the door a group of them walked up to Alex and Christ.

“You filthy rotten, cheating, bilge rat, where is all that gold you swindled from me last time ye were here?” One of them said as he pulled his sword.

“I won that game fair and square mate, no need fer hard feelings.” Alex returned, sounding as cocky as he was acting.

“Ya cheated and I know it.” He returned, pointing his finger at Alex.

Before Alex could protest anymore the man addressing him tightened his grip on his sword and swung it at Alex. Alex was barely able to pull his sword, blocking his swing as his sword came out of the scabbard. “Hey now, I did not cheat that card game, yer just a sore loser.” Alex said as he pulled his sword all the way out.

“Yer a lying pirate, why would anyone believe you!” He said as swung his sword down again.

Alex blocked it again. “So are you.” He answered pulling his sword away and swinging his fist hitting the man in the jaw.

The man dropped his sword then and lunged at Alex. They wrestled on the ground for a while until Alex got himself situated on top of him and started drilling his fists into the man.

Chris watched everything. At first the pirates that were with the man just stood there until Alex started pounding on the man. Then one of them decided to pull their sword. Christopher ran over and grabbed Alex's sword of the ground, running over and blocking the man from taking Alex's head off.

Chris fought as much as possible until the man pulled a dagger and stabbed into his ribs. Alex laid one more, well placed, hit on the man and jumped quickly to help Christopher. Before he knew it the rest of the crew were showing up, telling him to take Christopher and get him fixed up, so he did. He drug Christopher out of the middle of the fight and started to un-tuck his shirt. Christopher grabbed his hand then.

"Don't." He begged.

"Chris, I have to, you'll bleed out if I don't." Alex returned fighting to get his hand out of Christopher's grip.

"Then somewhere more private please." Christopher plead.

"This is ridiculous." Alex spat out.

"Please, you'll understand later."

Alex let out a deep breath and pulled Christopher up, helping him get to the nearest room. He paid for it and practically drug Christopher up to a bed. "Lock the door." Christopher demanded.

Alex had enough of his petty requests, but he knew if he didn't Christopher would keep arguing so he locked the door, then just ripped Christopher's shirt open. He stared at the material wrapped around his breasts, *her* breasts. He understood the feeling of closeness that he had towards her now.

"You're a woman." He yelled, more relieved than ever before to find out that a man was a woman.

"Shh..." Christopher returned. "You're Spanish."

He unwrapped the cloth that was hiding her breasts and warmed a metal plate in the fire and pressed it against the wound, he was almost surprised when she didn't scream as much as he was expecting. He waited for the pain to subside.

"So what's your real name?" He asked.

"Christina Walters." She answered. "What's yours?"

"I'm not the one that has been lying." Alex returned.

Christina started wrapping the fabric up so that it didn't get tangled, she needed to wash it now that it was covered with blood, and she also needed to sew it thanks to that damn pirate. "Yes you have been."

"It's Alexander Boseuilla." He answered.

"You're the rich man that went missing." She answered, rubbing her sore breasts.

He couldn't look away from her as she pulled her hat off and took the pins out that she had used to hold her hair up, letting all of her hair fall free, covering her breasts. She reminded him of a mermaid then. "Yes that's me." He answered, trying to get himself to look away.

"Why'd you leave, you had everything everyone could have dreamed of?" She asked.

"My mother and father were arses, I couldn't stand them. They wanted me to marry strictly for wealth and I couldn't do that, so I ran away." He stated. "So what's your story? The real one?"

"It was basically what I told you." She answered.

"That's not all of it though." He returned, raising an eyebrow.

"He tried to rape me, I fought with him, then hit him over the head with a lamp. I killed him." She said.

"Can't say I blame you." Alex returned taking off his shirt and handing it to Christina.

She put it on, he was kind of hoping she wouldn't. "I suppose I'll have to find another way to run now." She said seeming upset.

"Why?" He asked.

"I'll be marooned as soon as you tell the captain." She answered.

"Whoever said I was going to tell?" He returned.

"You'll be punished too if you don't." She stated as she got up and grabbed a rag to clean his eyebrow that was split open in the fight

"I'd rather be marooned with a woman than alone." He said.

She giggled. There was a pounding at the door then. "Hey mate, how be Christopher?"

"He's fine." Alex yelled.

"Let me in ta see him." Oliver's voice came booming through the door.

"I'm a bit busy mate." Alex returned.

"What ye got a woman in yer bed?" Oliver returned.

"Aye mate, quite a woman at that." He answered glancing back at Christina.

There was silence after that and they knew that Oliver had left. "So ye have never bedded anyone, ye just didn't want to admit it because it's not manly." He said.

"Actually that wasn't a lie, I'm not a noble woman, and I had no need to save myself for marriage." She answered.

"So tell me, what else have ye been hiding?" He questioned.

"That's it, I am a woman." She answered.

"You're also attracted to me." He returned.

"What makes you so sure?" She asked.

He started to move toward her more. "The way you steal looks at me whenever you can, the way you are staring at my bare chest." He started as he got directly in front of her. "The way you're not stopping me now." He added as he moved so that he would have been able to kiss her, she leant back, he continued on until he was directly over her, she was now laying back on the bed. Her eyes were wide, but she didn't look scared. He kissed her neck lightly. "Mainly it's the way you're not asking me to stop." He kissed her lips.

"What if I do?" She asked as his lips separated from hers.

"Then I'd stop." He answered, kissing her lips again.

She parted her lips for him, allowing him to take her in the most heated kiss she had ever had before. He started to move his hand down her body but she grabbed his hand and stopped him.

"Alex, I'm not ready." She said, trying to control her breaths.

CHAPTER 4

Christina woke up and practically jumped off the bed seeing Alex lying next to her, not wearing a shirt. She quickly lifted the blanket relieved to see his breeches still on. She thought back to last night, slightly panicking.

"Alex what did we do?" She yelled waking him up.

"God woman, must you be so loud." He returned, then sat up glancing around the room quickly. "Yer still dressed so if something happened it wasn't me."

"We woke up in bed together." She returned.

"There's only one bed in the room." He said.

"What the hell happened last night?" She asked, trying to remember.

She remembered him taking out a bottle of rum after she told him she wasn't ready. All she remembered was them drinking and laughing. The last thing she remembered was them playing a game of cards.

"I don't think anything happened, Chris." Alex said. "Let me go get you another shirt, so I can have mine back."

Christina didn't say anything she just watched as Alex got up and left, still trying to put together what happened last night. She remembered the fight outside of the tavern, and getting stabbed. She remembered Alex listening to all her ridiculous pleas for privacy before he even knew her secret, but why did he have to try to bed her the second he knew she was a woman? She was definitely going to ask him when he came back.

Of course then there was a knock at the room door. But instead of waiting for her to answer they just walked in. Alex tossed a shirt at her along with some more of the fabric that she used to hide her breasts. He then set a sword by the bed standing up.

"What's all this for?" She asked.

"Well the fabric you had before is covered in blood, same with the shirt, and if'n yer going to be a pirate ye need at least a sword." He answered abruptly.

"Why did you try to move so fast last night?" She asked.

"What do ya mean?" He asked.

"The second you could after you found out I was woman you were trying to bed me." She returned, agitated as she spoke.

"I think I've known for a while now, I just wasn't sure." He answered.

"How did you know?" She asked starting to panic a little about it.

"Honestly, it was just the way I was feeling about you, you never did much to give it away." He answered, running his hand across the top of his hair.

Her cheeks flared red, she knew she had been feeling a major attraction towards him but she had no idea that he felt the same, even when he thought she was a man. She got up and went into the bathroom to wrap herself up and give Alex his shirt back. As soon as she walked out he helped her put the scabbard and sword across her waist. As his hand slid across her hip she felt a sudden, lingering warmth fill her tummy.

"Ye sure are a more beautiful woman than ye are a man." He said.

She didn't answer, she pinned her hair up on top of her head and put her hat over it, relieved that she at least got to be somewhat of a woman last night. As soon as she put her hat on a few of the other crew members came barging through the door. "Captain Billy has recruited the men we need, he said screw the rest, we gots to go." Oliver said being the first one threw the door.

"What happened this time?" Alex asked.

"He and one of the merchants got into a lil squabble over some o' the goods we were selling, so captain took the money anyway." Oliver said.

"Shit." Alex mumbled as he tossed his own shirt back on and headed out the door. He knew the captain probably flipped his lid like he always did when it came to money. He always knew what he could get out of the stuff he was selling and would not be underpaid even if it wasn't much off.

They all ran to the ship, meeting up with Isaac and Hugh who were trying to drag the overly drunken James back to the ship before he could be left behind. The ship was already ready to sail by the time they got to the longboat but so was the merchant ship that Alex was sure was chasing after the red diamond.

They hopped in the longboat and hurriedly rowed to the red diamond. They quickly climbed up the rope ladder and pulled the longboat up, barely getting it in place before the merchant ship started to catch up to them. The merchant ship shot a cannon blast and barely missed the red diamond.

"Load the guns and shoot the bloody bilge rats!" Captain Billy yelled at the top of his lungs as he pulled his sword from his scabbard. He looked at the Navigator, "Take us and slam into them broadside I want that dirty cheat's ship at the bottom of the locker."

The red diamond slammed into the broadside of the gold doubloon just as a blast was coming from the cannons, leaving three great big holes in the gold doubloon. The ship started to back off then. Alex was relieved at that sight considering Chris still had that stab wound and he hadn't had the chance to teach her shit about sword fighting, although he was pretty sure she would catch on quickly.

"The bastards are running now, sent them packing real quick." James said as he stumbled across the deck.

"James go to bed, ye can be on a night watch tonight, ye drunken arse." Oliver said as lightly pushed James toward the barracks. “No vomiting in the hold either or you’ll clean the entire ship by yerself.”

Most the crew laughed as James muttered some drunken insults and stumbled down to the barracks to find his bed. He barely made it without falling. The rest of the crew quickly jumped to work on getting the ship going at full speed.

Alex avoided Christina as much as he could while he worked. He even got himself acquainted to the two new members of the ship, Pete and Xavier. He wasn’t as interested in their stories as he pretended to be though, he was more interested in his excitement in finding that Christopher was actually a woman, but now his heart pounded in his chest more and more every time he saw her stealing glances. He had to fight himself to keep himself from indulging in her luscious lips again.

By the time they got done adjusting the sails and tarring the deck there wasn’t much day left, so Alex decided to spend it teaching Christina to use her sword. He had her follow him down to the hold, just so he could teach her without anyone getting in their way, and or putting their two sense into the matter of how she fought. He had to make it really simple at first, considering her injuries he could only show her the proper ways to hold it and swing it, but he couldn’t go into the complicated stuff for a while.

For the next couple of weeks, he taught her to clean the sword probably and take care if it the right way so that it wouldn't break or rust. He'd have her swing it around as simply as possible so she would start working up the muscles she would need if they were to get into a bad sword fight.

When her wounds were healed he taught her to parry attacks and then got to start on showing her how to put her weight into her swings before dinner was announced as ready. He smiled at her when they started to put their swords up for the night. “Shall we continue this later tonight or just pick it up in the morning?” He asked trying awfully hard to charm her.

“We have to be up at the crack of dawn, didn't any of the new people get put in here?” She questioned.

Alex glanced around the other bunks. “Looks like it's still just you and me sweetheart.” He said winking.

Her cheeks flared red, was he going to be flirting with her the entire time now that he knew she was a woman? She was liking all the extra attention from him, but she wasn't sure if it was just because she was the only woman, thanks to the bar fight he wasn't able to be bedded by one of the wenches at the tavern, and their stay had been shortened due to Captain Billy being so greedy about a few measly pieces of eight.

She without a doubt had a major attraction to Alex, even before she knew that he was filthy rich running from his family. Deep down though, she knew that nothing could ever become of two people in hiding even if they were safely hidden under the black flag. Thinking about the word safely made her think about how much danger they were in all the time just being aboard the pirate ship, and how much more danger she would be in if anyone found out.

"There be a Merchant ship, Captain what do we do?" They heard come from the deck of the ship.

"Take her." Billy returned.

Alex and Chris ran out on deck then, their swords at the ready for a fight. They raised the black flag and the merchant ship started to turn around.

"She's running Captain." Oliver stated as if he couldn't already see that.

"Well chase her." Billy yelled.

They did. It took them maybe an hour to catch up and smash into the broadside of the merchant ship they were attacking. They raised their white flags, and all the men lined up on deck. The crew walked over the gangway, all of them except for Xavier, Pete, and Hugh.

Billy made her and Alex stay on the deck with the merchant crew as they all went down below to search for items of value to them. It was only moments before they could hear a woman's screams as Billy drug her out on deck. Christina's eyes opened in terror as Billy ripped her dress open.

One of the men from the merchant ship tried to stop him but Billy pulled out a pistol and shot him before he could even have a chance. The other men from the merchant ship raised their hands basically as a statement that they weren't going to try and stop him. Christina looked away and tried to drown out the screams of the poor woman. Alex did the same.

Before they knew it some of the other men were handing them the stuff they had grabbed and started to join in, either holding some of the men back or taking the woman as Billy did. Christina saw Oliver walk back over the gangway and she followed him. She dropped all of the stuff in her arms down on the deck and started to walk down to the barracks.

Oliver grabbed her shoulder. "It's a hard thing to watch Lad, I know." He started.

"How can he be so cruel to do that to someone, the wenches are one thing, cause they are willing to for pay but to take someone against their will like that it's disgusting." She said.

"I know, but if ye stand against him on it, he'll just shoot ye. I learned that the hard way." He said as he pulled his shirt up, showing a scar suggesting he had just barely been hit by the bullet. "Just walk away every time. It's better that way."

"Do they always do that?" She questioned.

"Only if there be a woman aboard the ship, and if someone tried to protect her, they get shot." Oliver started. "That be the only reason 'e ever uses that pistol. He's not the only one that does it either."

"I could never do anything like that to anyone." She answered.

"Ah lad, neither could I, and some of the other men aboard the ship, I've seen men puke after seeing him do it. I've puked after seeing him do it." Oliver started. "It gets easier when you learn to just dismiss it, go get yerself a heaping glass of rum, and just try to forget."

"Thank you." She said as she walked down to the barracks and grabbed the biggest glass she could find in the galley and filled it up to the top.

She sat in her room, realizing that she would never be safe, unless she was a man. She realized she would suffer the same fate as that woman if she was ever discovered, and it wouldn't be much better if she got caught on land, she would be hung immediately, at least she had a chance here.

Then she realized how much risk Alex was taking on by hiding her secret with her. She wished he would have never found out, because she knew that the pirate's aboard the ship, at least most of them would have their way with her before she was marooned and Alex would be marooned with her. She walked out the door and down to the galley to grab the food. Her face had gone pale with worry.

Heading back to the bunk-room to eat, she realized that she wanted to be left to solitude to figure out what she was going to do. She began to feel sick to her stomach and barely ate half the food she was served. She watched out the porthole for a while as they left the place that could have been her new hiding spot. She wished she would have thought of all of that while she was there, but then again she wasn't any better off on a pirate island either, plus her master was well known so she wouldn't be safe anywhere.

Alex walked into the room then breaking her of her thoughts. "What's wrong?" He asked calmly.

"I just realized what would happen if I get found out." She answered, refusing to look away from the porthole.

"What do you mean?" He asked, locking the door behind him. "You read the rules when you signed the articles how could you just realize that?"

"Not that, you see how pirates treat women, I'm one of them." She returned. "I saw the way a lot of the crew members were grabbing at the wenches in the tavern, it would be no better for me."

Alex walked over to her and made her look at him. "I won't let that happen, and I know a few others on the ship that would help me stop it. I would get you away safely even if it took my own life."

"I know there are good men on this ship, and I know some of them would try to stop it, but you saw what he did to the one on that ship that tried." She started. "I have grown close to plenty of men in this crew, and would never wish to see them harmed."

As the tears started to stream down her cheeks, Alex didn't know what to do so he just kissed her forehead and took her food out of the room leaving her to think about what she needed to think about. He didn't know what to say to her other than what he did but as she told him what she was afraid of he felt a terrible need to protect her, and he could more than see himself killing half the crew over her, it was like he could actually feel himself doing it as he thought about it happening.

He had been with this crew for over a year now, going on two, he knew some of them were foul and the others were respectable, but he wouldn't put it passed them to rape a woman if they found them on board, especially Christina, she was absolutely gorgeous, like a mermaid sent from Poseidon himself.

He pushed the thoughts out of his head, knowing he was actually getting angry over the thought of it. He filled his flask with rum and headed back to the bunkroom. He drank and drank from it, trying to get the angering thoughts out of his head.

Christina had already went to bed, he knew she was still awake, her sobs were quiet but he could still hear them, but he had no idea what to say to her. Unable to take her crying anymore he climbed into her bunk and pulled her against him. He ran his hand on her arm and whispered.

"Christina I will never let anything happen to you."

"Yeah but you could be killed then, and I am just not worth the trouble Alex." She kept her voice down.

He made her roll over to face him. "Chris, you are definitely worth the trouble." He stated as he took her lips in the kiss he had been longing for all day long.

He pulled away quickly. "Ye need to stop crying." He whispered. "If the men hear ye they'll get their suspicions." He wiped her tears for her and got off her bed, as soon as the sobbing stopped.

CHAPTER 5

Alex had spent all of his free time teaching Chris how to use a sword properly and effectively, then once that was over with and she could easily take down all the pirates on the ship he taught her hand to hand combat. He didn't leave out anything. He wanted her to be able to protect herself no matter what could possibly happen.

The more they spent time together the more he was falling for her. He was ready to make her his but he knew she was still frightened over the thought. She was so afraid that she would be discovered that she just refused him every time, telling him too much was at stake. The rejections got harder and harder for her, he could see it in her eyes every time, and he knew she shared the same feelings he did.

One day he just stopped asking. He knew how he felt about her, and it was more than anything he had ever felt before but he also knew that it was a lot at risk for her. He told the Captain that he didn't feel well that day, so he just stayed down in the bunkroom. His head was throbbing from all the drinking he did the night before. He didn't feel right about letting Chris be up on the deck by herself but he knew that the entire crew had no idea that she was a woman.

He was ready to just stay in his room all day until he heard the words he had feared so badly yelled out on deck. “Black flag Captn.” Immediately after there was hustle and bustle, clinging and clamoring, as the crew grabbed their weapons from below. Jumping out of bed he grabbed his and Chris’ swords, running out of the room just before a shot was laid to the side of the red diamond, barely able to keep his footing as he ran, he tossed Christina’s sword to her as he came out on deck, just in time to see the other ship slam into them, knocking half of them over. Just as he caught his footing the red diamond shot at the other ship.

As the shots hit the ship, men swung over on lines, landing on deck planning for a takeover. Alex stood his ground until he saw a few people surrounding Christina. He went after them, stabbing one from behind, he pulled his blade out just in time to parry another one’s swing. Swing for swing the man matched his movements just in time to save himself until Alex finally kicked his foot out knocking the man back. He swung his sword while the man tried to catch his footing, chopping deep into his side, Alex turned back to Christina not taking the time to see if the man had died or not.

Alex turned just in time to see Christina get her first kill on board, and it seemed to traumatize her more than he thought it would. He had figured since it wasn’t the first time she had killed anyone it wouldn't be so hard on her but he could read it on her face that she was mortified, she certainly could handle her own though, which made him proud.

Footsteps approaching behind him broke him of his thoughts and he ducked down just in time to be missed by the hearty blow. He returned the swing as he came back up taking the intruder down with little effort. He turned again quickly to see two more limp bodies lying by Christina's feet. The other crew started retreating quickly, with maybe five of them left out of the entire crew.

"Follow them o'er and take all their shit." Captain Billy yelled.

Most the crew did, others just threw the intruders bodies off the ship. Alex was amazed to see that there were no serious injuries on any of the crew, that usually never happened, but they all had been getting better with their battle tactics, especially considering that Billy and the red diamond never backed down from a fight. He had seen many battles aboard this ship, and not once had they lost. Once the bodies were thrown off the deck of the ship some people got to work on cleaning up the blood while others got to work on patching the hole that was down in the barracks. They worked late into the night until the hole was patched enough to make it to port so it could properly be fixed.

Captain Billy was shocked that the other ship had very little food aboard, barely enough to feed one man, which would explain why they attacked, pirates rarely attacked other pirates unless they needed to. However they had tons of stuff worth money, just nothing to feed them. He was glad to take all their loot, as were the other men of the crew. Oliver was happy to take down all the items and put a price on them splitting everything between the members and handing the paper to Billy for him to pay the crew when they got the money. The crewmen tried not to pay much attention as they did this so they continued on their work.

Exhausted as they were, all the men headed off to bed as soon as everything was done, not saying a word outside of goodnight. Christina was already sleeping when Alex walked into the room which kind of made him sad. He was hoping to get to talk to her before they fell asleep but the deck was clean before the hole was patched so she got to go to bed before him. He just laid down in his bed and hoped he would get to talk to her in the morning. He wanted to tell her how well she did in the fight, he was amazed at how great she did for her first pirate fight, but that would all have to wait for the morning to come.

When Alex woke, Christina was already out on deck, doing the usual morning duties that she had claimed for her own. She was the best at them so that's what she always did, swabbing the deck and re-tarring the floorboards, then sometimes if she had the time she would go down and help the cook with breakfast and washing the dishes. She wasn't supposed to be doing the cabin boy duties anymore but Alex was sure that she had taken a liking to them because they were pretty close to what she was doing before she had taken refuge under the black flag of the red diamond.

"Alex." Captain Billy yelled, breaking him from his musings.

"Yes Captain?" He asked.

"Take the two new boys down to the hold and start teaching them to use a sword, they were terrible yesterday, they got lucky that the other crew was worse." Billy yelled, shoving the two new crewmembers toward Alex.

He did what he was told, finding little to no excitement in teaching them, compared to the excitement he found in spending his time with Christina. The entire time he was teaching them he kept thinking about his training with Christina, she was much smoother when she swung a blade and her movements seemed to flow like the ocean itself. These two were sloppy and almost careless about what they would hit. They barely made it out without breaking anything with value. He decided to make the best of it though considering he would be there teaching them for about a week as Captain Billy would want him too.

While he was training the two new men he found that the only real time he got to spend with Christina was the meal times aboard the ship, which felt like it was tearing him apart on the inside. Wondering if she felt the same, he didn't dare bother to tell her how he was feeling. Every night since he started training those to landlubbers he just went straight to bed when they were done for the day, and before he even knew it they were making port at Port Royal to take care of the necessary things aboard the ship. Finally he and Christina could spend some time together since he knew it would take one day to patch the hole in the ship and that Billy would give them at least one day to have fun in town after its done, although he usually gave them more time than that.

Chris was acting weird as the Master Carpenter was yelling out who he wanted to help him patch the hole. Alex was surprised when Isaac didn't call his name out, but instead called out Pete and Xavier, along with Adam, Henry, James and Martin. Alex figured he called out Pete and Xavier since they were new to the ship and he wanted to test them out and see if they were better than they looked at anything, especially since no body had seen any skill from the two of them.

Alex got onto a longboat with Chris and rowed into town with her. They were quiet aboard the longboat, but there were others on it too, so they couldn't risk speaking without any privacy. He could see how worried she was to be there, although he wasn't sure why, considering it wasn't Barbados he didn't think she had a reason to be nervous but upon walking into the town he could hear all the gossip about a noble man killed and a servant woman hiding. Once the crew that was on the longboat with them disappeared he grabbed her hand and pulled her into an alleyway next to the tavern.

"Are they talking about you?" He questioned, already knowing the answer.

She nodded.

"On the off chance that someone may figure ye out, I'll go get us a room and we'll just stay there until we be ready ta leave." He said as he started walking towards an inn.

Christina followed him to the inn and tried to stay away from anyone that might be able to recognize her. She was impatient as she waited for him to get the room but quickly followed him to it as soon as he had it paid for. She locked the door as soon as they got into the room. She tried to pay him back for it but he refused the money. She went into the bathroom and took off the fabric hiding her breasts. She took her hair down shaking it out. She walked back out.

"Why don't you go to the tavern with the rest of the crew?" She asked, seeing that Alex was already getting antsy.

"Because you can't." He answered bluntly.

"I'll be fine, as long as I stay here." She answered.

"I'd rather be here to make sure." He said as he walked over to her. He kissed her lips, not even waiting for a cue. "I'd rather know that you are safe than just thinking you are."

"But you…" She started.

He kissed her again to keep her from arguing. "Christina I would rather, be here just kissing you than be there with another woman, or getting drunk with the crew. I thought I made meself clear on that."

Taken breathless by his sweet words she practically melted in his arms. Hearing him say it was different on the ship, when it wasn't an option, but saying it when it was just melted her inside and out. Her heart, along with the rest of her body was tingling from the kind, loving words, and she hadn't even touched him yet. He pulled out a flask and handed it to her. Watching her drink it as he would have, he smiled at her as he usually did.

He pulled out his cards that he always seemed to carry whenever on land and began to shuffle them. "What game do ye want to play milady?"

She took the cards from him and set them down. "Tell me, why are you so sweet to me, when I've only refused you and what you want?" She questioned.

"It's just somethin' about ye that has me a tangled mess." He answered.

"Tell me." She asked.

"I'd show ye if you'd let me." He returned.

Looking down at the ground, her cheeks started to heat up, and even more so as he lifted her chin with his finger, taking her lips in a passionate, forceful kiss that made her heart leap into her throat as she melted even more into him.

His touches were like fire sweeping across her skin, awakening the burning desire she hadn't felt in so long as he moved his hand to her neck. Kissing her as if he wanted to steal the very breath from her lungs and leaving her panting and gasping for oxygen as if they had been engulfed in the waters that seemed to be their prison, yet their savior. He started to move her towards the bed, but she felt no regrets as they lay down, his hands roaming every portion of her body, peaking her interest more than ever before, stripping her clothes off of her as he went.

She didn't refuse when he followed his hands with his mouth. She felt the excitement of the storm yet the calm of the lifeless waters as he started to strip himself of every article of clothing he wore. Her stomach felt as uneasy as the tide as he started to lay on top of her but the second his lips took hold of hers again the threatening waves stopped. As he pushed into her she felt a warmth inside and out accompanied by an overwhelming shudder through her entire body. Her senses were more alive than ever, but she barely even noticed when he moved so that she was straddling his hips tightly.

Before she could even start to move his hands and lips were roaming her body again, then he started to guide her movements. He took her lips again, with so much passion she would swear he was in love with her. Then a feeling arose, something she never felt before but for a second it was as if she was being surrounded by a flowing river then everything disappeared into a peaceful bliss. Her body was numb inside and out, all she could feel was her heart beating and the sweet tender kisses Alex was laying upon her chest.

He rolled so she was lying next to him, still conjoined. He ran his hand up and down her bare thigh as he pulled out. "See it's a tangled mess." He panted.

"Aye that it is." She said kissing his lips with all the passion he had made her feel. Her heart was beating so loudly she felt it was going to come out of her chest.

"So ye will be mine?" He asked again running his hand up her arm.

"I can't... It's too risky." She answered.

"It's just as much risk as yer taking now." He returned. "I'm not going to be kissing on ye in front of the entire ship."

"Do you really want to take that risk?" She asked.

"I'd take the risk of going out to sea without a ship fer ye lass." He answered, flashing her a charming smile.

"Alright I guess we can give it a chance." She returned not too sure about her answer.

"Are ye hungry?" He asked getting up and putting his breeches on.

She nodded, they hadn't eaten since breakfast and it was already late.

"I'll go get us some food fer right now." He answered.

She put her clothes back on, not realizing how weak her legs were until she stood up. By the time she managed to get all of her clothing back on, Alex was back with a big plate of food for each of them. He set it all down at the table and they started to eat, quietly at first until there was a knock at the door. "What?" Alex asked.

"Captain said we are going after the Spanish treasure yer always talking about, he wants ye to help Henry map it out in the morning." Richard's voice boomed through the door.

"Alright." He answered, and waited to hear footsteps.

"What treasure is he talking about?" Christina asked curiously.

"It's called Prohibido Saqueo, or you might have heard of it as the Forbidden plunder." Alex answered.

"I actually haven't heard anything about it, is there a story behind it?" She asked.

"Yeah, umm, it was a treasure shared by two lovers." Alex started. "Their parents refused to let them be together. The woman was rich beyond all belief and the man was just a merchant sailor. When they finally asked the parents the answer was no, but they snuck around with each other, still trying to hold up the relationship. They got caught one day and the father of the woman sent her away. When the man found out about it, he stole his own family's ship and went after her, they lived a life as pirates and lived as kings and queens condemned to the same waters as us. But the woman's family found where they were one day and blew the ship to smithereens, it's said that all their wealth lies in the harbor of an uncharted island somewhere north of Veracruz, and It would be enough for the hole crew to live as kings."

"Have you thought about leaving the pirate life since you've been here?" She asked, looking at the table.

"Yeah, I have, but I love the sea now, if I did ever leave piracy I'd probably want to do something like work on a merchant ship or for the navy. Why?" He answered.

"I still haven't figured out what I want to do." She returned, sighing her disappointment. "I can't ever go back to Barbados, I'm not supposed to be on a pirate ship, I wanted to have a family one day, but with what I am doing right now my life is always at risk. I have no place left in this world and I am sure if they found out I was a woman that I would die on whatever sad desolate island that they left me on."

"Aye, belay that nonsense, ye know I would be there with ye to get you back to civilization and make sure ye survive it." Alex answered. "I think the question is what would you want to do when that happens?"

"I've actually come to enjoy life at sea, it's very peaceful, even with all the pirate battles and everything going on." She answered.

"Well then, when we get the Prohibido Saqueo we will buy a ship, and ye can be me pirate queen, laced up like all the other women with beauty that don't even hold a candle to you." Alex answered.

Her cheeks flared red at his kind words. Her stomach felt knotted up every time he complimented her like that. She felt a nervousness at the thought of them running a ship together though. "How would we even know how to be the captain of a pirate ship though? I've only been a pirate for a few months now and still have to concentrate on everything I do." She stated, fiddling with her hands nervously.

"You'd be perfect for it, see cause you already think ahead to what could and couldn't happen and you weigh the options better than anyone I know, The main thing about being captain is that it's relentless and everything you do has a consequence, you run the ship and the people on it and you already look at all that shit anyway so it shouldn't be too hard for you to get accustomed to the fact that all of our lives will be in your hands. The quarter master has to split the pay evenly among the crew members. Then there is the Bosun who basically makes sure that the captain is obeyed. The captain's job is the hardest, with all of the emotional strain." Alex returned. He walked around to the part of the table she was sitting at and took her hand. “Ye would be me queen, and I yer king. Ye would be me queen of the seas.”

“That does sounds wonderful and stressful all at the same time, plus you have forgotten one thing.” She returned.

“What’s that?” He questioned.

“How would we get a crew?” She asked.

“I know a few people that want to leave Captain Billy’s ship. They don’t like the way he just stands there and barks orders, he doesn’t put anyone’s well-being into the matter.” He answered. “Then we could sail to Tortuga and pick up as many people as we need, and make sure that they understand the articles of agreement.”

“We will need a navigator though too.” She returned.

“Nah, Henry wants to leave, says the navigator should be paid extra too.” Alex answered. “I do agree, he is amazing at what he does and never gets us lost or veered off track.”

“So what, we’re going to mutiny or something, or we just going to wait until we make port after we get the treasure?” She asked.

“A mutiny is too much risk with how many people like Billy, and I don’t have a problem with him, so I don’t want to hurt him, so we will wait until we make port and get paid for everything.” He stated.

“Alright,” she answered, barely able to contain the excitement she had.

“Until then, my beauty, ye will have ta keep yer amazing body, hidden behind a man’s clothes.” He said as he kissed her knuckles. “It’s a shame that someone so beautiful, has to hide behind the clothes of a man, underneath a black flag.”

Her knees were already weak from his kind words, but he swept her up into his arms and laid her back down on the bed trailing kisses along her neck.

CHAPTER 6

When Christina woke up she was in the bed alone, bare again. She was still breathless from the night before. She wished Alex was still there with her but he had to work with Henry about mapping out the way to the Forbidden Plunder. She had no clue if Captain Billy would be there or not so she didn't know if he was going to talk to Henry about their plans to leave. However, she got up and got dressed as a man again.

Putting the clothing on and wrapping herself up just made her wish that she and Alex's plans would happen faster. She walked out of the room and headed to the ship to get her pay from the pirate ship they had to plunder. She apparently wasn't the only one headed that way, half of the crew was headed back, all of them talking about what they would be spending their money on while they were at port. She lied about what she was planning on doing with it, she told them all that she was going to get drunker than James usually got. Her real intentions were to save the money so they could get more stuff when they got their ship.

When they all got aboard the ship the quarter master had paper and a quill in his hand, sitting at the desk in the captain's cabin. The money was all separated into decent sized bags. As the crewmembers walked up one by one to get their pay, he put a check mark by their name, there were several marks by some of the names, then there was Christopher written there, she had earned her first pay and as he told her how much she had gotten, her mouth almost dropped to the floor.

"Yeah a lot of the new members have that reaction the first time we get in a big haul like that." Oliver stated. "The pay won't always be that great though, sometimes we don't even get enough to pay the crew, outside of buying food and supplies for the ship."

"Does the crew ever riot over that?" She asked, focusing more on trying to sound like a man than the money.

"Well someone did once, but when they did, Captain Billy took him down, had to keelhaul him, and then the crew got to split his earnins because he created a great big fuss o'er it, like he 'ad been a pirate his entire life." Oliver chuckled as he spoke about it.

"That sounds horrible." Chris answered.

"It was fer him, he didn't even make it halfway through, there were so many barnacles on the bottom of the ship, he was ripped wide open and bled out quicker than shit." He said. "Anyways get on to doin what ye got planned I got to get me business done afore too long so me can go get me a wench afore the morning comes." He said shooing her away from the desk quickly.

She walked down to the barracks and went into the bunkroom to see that there were some clothes thrown up on another bunk. She was almost disappointed to see that there would be someone in there with her and Alex, she had come to enjoy the privacy she had. The door opened and Alex walked in with a blonde man right behind him. "Ah perfect." Alex said at the sight of Chris.

"Tyler this is Christopher, but he likes to just be called Chris." He added.

Tyler put his hand out and shook Chris's hand. "Nice to meet you."

"Tyler was a friend of mine on the merchant ship before I joined Billy's crew. He's a good man, and almost good with a blade." He joked.

"Are you done helping Henry?" Christina asked.

"Yes we just finished the charts to where we be headin' and I was getting' ready to get me pay and find ye." Alex answered.

"I thought we were going to the tavern." Tyler returned.

"Yeah, but I told ye I'd have to get 'im first." Alex returned.

Christina didn't argue, she waited for them to leave the room and hid most of her coins in her duffle bag. She needed to get more clothes though, she only had two pairs now, and only one pair of breeches that didn't even fit her. She would go get more eventually, she just didn't know when. She went out of the room and caught up with Alex and Tyler, barely in time to get in the longboat with them.

She didn't really want to go to the tavern, but she knew if she argued it the crew would have their suspicions and since there was a couple more of the crew members in the longboat she didn't say or even act like she didn't want to go. She barely listened as Tyler and Alex were talking about the time they spent on the merchant ship together.

Walking into the tavern the smoke surrounded her along with the foul stench of sweat and vomit. The tavern looked hazy as she walked in but when her eyes adjusted it got better, slightly. She hated the smell of taverns but she didn't dare say anything with the majority of the crew there. She walked to the empty table towards the back door and waited for a bar wench to walk up.

Like the first time the wench sat on her lap and rubbed on her face as if she was a man. She pushed her off her lap. "Why don't ye go get us all an ale and call it good for now, lass?" She said, handing the wench the coins for it.

The wench pouted as she walked away. She was soon replaced by a redheaded one with the brightest red lips she had ever seen. Her hair was put up beautifully on her head as she walked over. She sat on Alex's lap and rubbed her hand up his chest.

"Oh Alex, I thought I would never see you again." She said, pressing kisses against his cheek.

“Heather, I didn’t know you still worked here.” He stated obviously stunned.

“Why would I leave here, when I know you’d always find me here?” She answered, moving so that her breasts were pressed up against his chest.

Christina tried to keep her temper under control but she was about ready to grab the bitch by her hair and drag her outside. She cleared her throat loud enough for Alex to hear her. Heather looked at her like she was insulted. “Come Alex, let’s go somewhere more private so we can get… more personal.” She said, taking his hand and rubbing it on her chest.

“Ah Heather, sadly, I have no interest in you today.” He said pulling his hand away from her.

“The way I had you moaning last time, would suggest differently.” She stated as she placed her hands on his thighs, leaning over so that her breasts were about ready to pop out completely.

“Heather really, go.” He said, noticing that Christina was chewing on her lip, her arms crossed and her fists balled as if she was ready to start swinging.

“Well come find me if you change your mind.” She said finally leaving. She blew him a kiss before she walked away.

“Chris.” Alex said.

She turned her head to face away from him. She didn’t care if the crew saw what she was doing, she was pissed. She waited for her ale since she had already paid for it. Once it got there she chugged it and left, not saying a word to Alex. She couldn't believe him, he could have at least pushed her off or something. She went back to the room and took off the damn fabric that held her breasts so tightly against her chest. He walked through the door about the time she had put her shirt back on.

"Holy shit, she's a woman." Tyler said.

"Why did you just run off like that?" Alex asked as he shut and locked the door behind him.

"Because I really don't like you letting those bar whores touch you in ways only I should be. I thought you were serious when you were talking to me last night, but apparently I was wrong as always." She crossed her arms over her chest.

"I got her off of me." He answered.

"Yeah after she rubbed all over you and you got a good face full of her chest, you dirty rotten pirate." She yelled.

"I could go sleep with her if that would make ye feel better." He returned. "I meant everything I said to you."

"It doesn't seem like it." She returned.

"Why didn't you tell me she's a woman?" Tyler interrupted.

"Christina, you can't be serious." Alex returned. "I would have told Billy about you if I didn't care so much."

"Could have fooled me." She returned turning to face away from him.

He chuckled. "I didn't know you were the jealous type."

"So." She spat back. "I didn't know you were the cheating type."

"I won't let another wench touch me, I promise, I thought we were trying to keep up appearances though." He answered.

She turned and looked at him. "What do you mean by that?"

"If you get caught as a woman, we both get marooned, remember, and now poor Tyler will too, but if he tells your secret I will kill him, so he best be keeping our little secret. If'n I would have pushed that wench away any sooner the crew would have been suspicious, and you've been pushin' them away." Alex explained.

"I guess that's true, but no more dammit." She returned trying to stay angry.

Alex walked over and kissed her lips. As soon as he kissed her the anger just flowed out of her and she almost forgot why she was even mad. "Me amour, ye be the only woman that be woman enough for me." He whispered in her ear. Her head spun from the exotic sound of the words he had used. Me amour, that meant my love. Her head was spinning faster and faster.

"So what is actually going on here?" Tyler asked.

"Christina is the woman I love, and if she is found out she will be marooned onto an island. So we must keep her secret." Alex answered.

"So who are you really?" Tyler asked. "I know you're not who you say you are either, you're speaking Spanish."

"My Name is Alexander Boseuilla." He answered.

"So the entire country of Spain is looking for you, and let me guess the woman is hiding because she has murdered someone?" His question was rhetorical.

"Actually yes, I am the servant that went missing after my master's death." She answered. "But I didn't mean to kill him, I was just trying to get him off of me." She forced tears to fall down her cheeks. "Please don't turn me in."

"Alex would kill me, remember?" Tyler let out a big sigh.

She dried her tears. "Thank you." Not even looking like she had cried at all. She smiled brightly, then turned to Alex. "I want you to cut my hair short." She said taking off her hat and letting her hair fall.

"Ye sure about that, love?" He asked.

"Yes." She answered.

He grabbed the dagger he kept in the waistband of his breeches and held her hair tightly as he sliced his dagger through it, cutting it, then letting it all fall to the floor. "I'm gonna miss that pretty hair of yours, even though I barely get to see it." He said.

"It'll grow back." She answered as she put her hat back on. She looked in the mirror then, she still looked the same, but at least now she could walk around without a hat. "What time do we leave tomorrow?"

"First thing in the morning." Alex stated.

"I should go get at least one more pair of breeches." She said and headed towards the door.

"I'll go get ye some clothes, remember yer still a wanted woman whether or not ye be dressed like a man." Alex returned. "Tyler can stay here and protect you for me."

He was out the door before either of them could protest. She looked at Tyler who still seemed to be staring at her chest. "You don't have to stay if you don't want to I can protect myself fine."

"Isn't it painful to hide those?" He asked pointing.

"Yes it is, very painful." She answered almost irritated.

"How do you do it?" He asked.

"I wrap a fabric around it so tight that I can barely breathe." She answered.

"So what are you going to do? Like before you get caught. I read the articles and I think you should do something before you do get caught."

"Well Alex and I are going to buy a ship from what he says." Christina answered.

"That still doesn't help the risk though, what if some pirates invade and take you captive, or what if you're found out before then?" Tyler asked.

"I don't know, I guess we never really thought that far. I didn't know pirates took people captive." She answered.

"That's how Alex became a pirate, Captain Billy told him it was either join the ship or die." He answered.

"I am good with a sword and can fight with my hands also, I guess I'd just defended myself the best I could if that happened." She returned.

He didn't say anything else he just sat down at the table and stayed quiet until Alex walked through the door, handing Christina a new outfit. She thanked him then noticed that he had food in his hands, she was hungry, they hadn't eaten all day, so when he set it all down and started making sandwiches for them all she could feel her stomach growling. She thanked him when he handed her the sandwich and she sat down to eat.

Alex explained their plan a bit better to Tyler, she felt relieved when he agreed to join them, once the Prohibido Saqueo was squandered. He even said he'd put some of his earnings towards the ship. She was also shocked to find out that Henry agreed to join with the pay that Alex offered, which was one and a quarter shares instead of just one. So they already had four members ready to go, that would at least be able to get them to Tortuga for more members.

Their plans were coming along great already and they still had at least a month before they could live them out, but as Christina and Alex went to bed that night, she felt a relief in knowing that Alex was really serious about what he had said to her. She couldn't wait till morning when they would board the ship and sail on to their new horizons.

CHAPTER 7

The sailing had been smooth for a week, but there was finally a storm rolling in which was almost a relief from how calm and uneventful the journey had been so far. Alex watched the darkened clouds as the lightning cracked down on the ocean. Ah, yes the storms on the ocean were always a beautiful sight to see, until the storm was in the ship's path, then it got brutal and very tiring, sometimes they would even lose crew members. He was worried sick about Christina but they were almost to where they were headed. The wind had been on their side the entire time which put them ahead of time, but the storm was about ready to make them lose hours of time and could possibly veer them off track.

The entire crew stood on deck waiting, they had all pulled the sails in and tied them to the masts so they wouldn't rip too bad. Isaac had ran through the ship making sure that the boat wouldn't have any leaks. The crew members were all wearing their thick coats, except him, he had given his thickest to Christina, and he was just wearing a regular coat. They were bracing themselves the best they could, the storm was coming towards them pretty quickly.

They had buckets ready, and they all had lines tied around their waists this time. The guns in the hold were all tied down so they wouldn't roll around the ship. A lightning strike hit the waters next to the ship barely missing the ship but creating a stir in the water.

It was just a few more minutes until the storm hit them full blast, rain was pounding on the deck of the ship and the water from the waves of the ocean were crashing on the deck too. The crew started shoveling off the water with the buckets, but Alex stayed ready for whatever else would come, and before he knew it he was climbing up the masts to secure the lines around the sails better.

It seemed like hours before they hit the eye of the storm, but so far it hadn't turned the ship around too much, however the crew was exhausted already and not many of them were able to keep their footing most the time. However, the hour they got of a break seemed to energize them as they all got a sip of the grogg from underneath and they were back at it as soon as the last part of the storm rolled in.

The crew was on top of everything for at least the first couple hours but the last of the storm got even worse and they started to fall behind, especially with some of the new members going overboard, a lot of them were trying to pull them up before they could die in the raging sea waters. The work went on for hours after the storm passed, and they barely got to bed before dawn.

They all slept in late that day, they all actually got to sleep until noon, but were still beat, muscles sore and aching, bodies bruised and battered, they all drug their feet getting back to work. After that storm though Alex was surprised that they still had the entire crew. One of the ones that fell off didn't have their line secured and Henry had to jump in after him, barely getting to him before he got drug underneath the ship, which would have been a horrid display, but at least now it was all over with.

Once they got the sails back down it was easy sailing for the day, other than the new men having to tar the deck. The rest of them just relaxed on the ship until something needed to be done. Christina had gotten sick so she stayed down in the bunk room so the rest of the crew wouldn't catch it. Truth was it was probably just from the storm and she would be better in the morning. However, Alex was taking her tea with lemon and honey in it, just to help her feel better. Hugh had made a stew for everyone to last throughout the day, which was wonderful considering the weather yesterday.

The day seemed to drag on though, but at least it wasn't all that hot, and not to cold either, the weather was actually perfect for once. However, they did still have another week to go before they got to where they needed to be, and the entire crew was ready to make port at the first place possible. Captain Billy refused to stop though, he had his eyes on a prize and refused to take them off.

He rushed the crew the next few days until the island was in clear view. He sent the crew to bed early that night so that they could all be up as soon as the anchor was dropped. The crew was sketchy about what was going to happen as soon as they got the treasure. All the people that knew about Alex's plans met in his room that night to plan what they were doing. Out of all the crew members they had at least half, including Oliver.

Alex was shocked when Oliver walked into the room, he was the very last one in there. He walked straight up to Chris and looked her dead in the eye. "Alright, Lassie, We are mutinying against the captain, but only because I know what exactly will happen to you if found out, I have seen it before and I am not willing to see it again, along with a lot of the other landlubbers that seem to enjoy Billy so much, and the only reason that I agree with you being the captain is because I dare not step on the other end of yer man's blade. So Pirate Queen, lead the way."

"How did you know I was a woman?" She asked.

"I was the first slave to run from him." He answered. "He raped and killed me maw, but I was there when they first brought you. That was the night I left. I remember seeing you before I left."

"How do you all want to do this? We weren't planning on a mutiny we were planning on just disappearing after the prize." Alex started. "Still think we should wait and just buy a ship."

"It'd be better if we mutinied, we have enough people, I made sure to tell the ones that I knew would be up for mutiny, and we can't let Billy keep doing the things he's doing, someone has to stop him." Henry said.

"Wait until the lights go out and make your move, keep the lass safe." Oliver returned. "Honestly I would have said do it during the storm but I didn't know what was goin' on then."

The bunk room door came flying off its hinges then. Billy stormed in and grabbed Chris by her arm pulling her on to the deck, ripping her shirt open as he got her up on deck. Alex came running up and knocked Billy to the floor, not meaning to knock Christina down with him. She hit her head off the deck hard enough to knock herself out. Alex pulled his sword out and swung it at Billy. Billy kicked the sword back with his boots, and got up quickly before Alex could swing again. He pulled his sword out just in time to block another swing.

Alex heard Christina scream and kicked Billy back, looking to see what was going on with Christina. Alex turned just in time to see Tyler cut down Richard, to get Christina free from his grasp. He heard Billy's footsteps and was able to duck under the blade quickly, and kick his feet out from underneath him, kicking Billy back so far he almost went overboard. Alex caught Billy off guard and rammed his sword into Billy's gut. Billy went for one last swing, and cut into Alex's shoulder pretty deep.

As Billy lay on the deck, spilling his blood all over the floorboards, the rest of the crew had rounded up Billy's other favorites tying them up. George, James, Richard and Billy were the only ones that died, but Clarence, Adam, John and Martin were forced to the brig until they were ready to sign the articles.

Alex looked over Christina, seeing she had a scratch on her face he slid some hair back behind her ear and kissed her lips. She saw his arm all bloodied and her face went pale.

"We should stitch you up." She said as she led him to the captain's cabin.

Tyler stopped her. "I'll stitch him up Captain, you need to get yer new articles written."

"I want everyone to have a say on that." She said.

"Don't ye think ye should get everyone in here then?" Alex asked.

"Deck is cleaned up, Captain." Oliver said as he walked through the door.

"Alright, send everyone in, I want them all to have a say in the articles, and what position who takes." She said.

"No offense meant Captain, but ye need to sound more demandin'." Oliver stated.

"Get everyone in here now!" She yelled.

"Aye Captain." Oliver said as he walked out onto the deck.

Moments later the entire crew from the mutiny was in there. Oliver grabbed the book that had the articles written down in it and a quill with ink. He set it down in front of Christina. "First thing is first, the pay. I think it should be more equal, like what about one and a half shares for all people aboard the ship with the crew for more than six months people before that get one and a quarter." She asked.

"The captain still deserves more, two shares for the captain." Oliver stated.

The crew men agreed.

"No smoking in the hold at all?" She asked.

Alex had taken the book and started writing it down as they all discussed what they wanted to be on the articles. It took them nearly two hours to get them all in order but the crew was happy and so was Christina.

Articles Of Agreement

I. Every Man Shall obey civil Command; the Captain shall have two shares of all Prizes; every crew member aboard the ship for more than six months will receive one and a half shares, New members shall receive one and a quarter.

II. If any Man shall offer to run away, or keep any Secret from the Company, he shall be marooned with one Bottle of Powder, one Bottle of Water, one small Arm, and Shot.

III. If any Man shall steal anything in the Company, or game, to the Value of a Piece of Eight, he shall be marooned or shot.

IV. No fighting on the ship, unless it be to learn. If found fighting aboard the ship and warned by the Captain or any other man in the company if the fighting shall not cease offenders will be thrown in the brig until they have calmed. If the fighting continues the crew shall vote on the punishment.

V. That Man that shall strike another whilst these Articles are in force, shall receive Moses' Law (that is, 40 Lashes lacking one) on the bare Back.

VI. No Smoking in the hold.

VII. No woman shall be harmed aboard this ship. If one is the offender will be Keelhauled or shot.

"I think Oliver should stay as the quartermaster, since he was always fair when Billy was the captain." Christina stated. "So vote."

Most the crew voted yes so Oliver remained the quartermaster. "Tyler as the Bosun?" She suggested.

That vote was easy, everyone voted yes to that. She continued down the line, until all the main jobs were taken up. Hugh would remain in the kitchen since he was a great cook, Alex would take over as the surgeon since he knew more about it than anyone else. Pete would be the master gunner, and Xavier would take over as the sail maker and assist Alex when needed. Henry would remain the navigator since he was the best any of them had seen.

"Should we go get our treasure or see if the others want to join now?" She asked. "If we go get the treasure now we'd have to come back, if we ask them now, we have a chance at hunting for food and scouting the island out."

"I'll go ask if they want to sign." Tyler returned.

Minutes later he returned with Philip, Clarence, and Martin. Christina went into the cabin real quick and took off the fabric that flattened her chest. She felt instant relief. She walked out of the cabin just as the men were finishing up signing the articles. She decided then that she didn't want the articles posted on the mast she wanted them left in the book, so she could know the people signing them better.

"Alright ye scallywags let's get the hell over there." She said as she walked towards the longboats. The men came over fairly quickly, just not as quickly as she was expecting. They searched the island for the treasure until they found a cave hidden by a huge waterfall. Alex was the first to go in, but once he hollered for them they all followed. They walked through a tunnel laid out with plenty of skeletons, some old some not, and a body that looked like a beast with a sword through it, while another body laid close by, they continued on, despite the dangerous look of the cave. As soon as they came to the end of the tunnel and to the hollowed out cave they were blinded by all the treasures in there, from coins to gems, it was definitely a pirate's dream. Not to mention, there were clothes and it was set up for a long stay if needed.

Oliver walked over to Christina, carrying a chest of clothes. "They aren't ruined and a lot better than the men's clothes you are wearing now." He said.

"Is everyone alright with me being a woman?" She asked.

"No one really cares as long as you're not soft, like most women." He said. "Plus if they argue, we'll just keelhaul them, or throw them overboard for the locker to take them."

She smiled. "Thank you, it's nice to not hide who I am. Now you dirty ole bilge rats, get all this plunder on the ship and Hugh can start hunting for some good meat." She demanded. Looking at Alex she realized he just stood there. She handed him the chest of clothing. "Come on now, get that all to the Captain's cabin."

He chuckled, until she raised an eyebrow then he started going. "Dump the chest out and bring it back for us to use to carry more gold." She demanded as she started lining her pockets with everything she could fit in them.

The crew laughed for minute as they continued out. It took them almost the entire night to carry out everything, and load it onto the ship. Christina helped the entire time, and by the time they were all done, Hugh had dinner cooked for them. They would eat, rest for the night and head to Tortuga to get more crew members.

Before they could reach Tortuga a ship was spotted. It didn't have its black raised so there was no telling if it was a merchant ship or not. However, it followed them all the way to Tortuga, disappearing every once in a while but it would be back after a few hours. They figured it was just a merchant ship, trying to find its way so they left it alone.

Once they all got to Tortuga Oliver went and traded everything for money and split it all up. He was shocked at how much money there was left after all the repairs to the ship. Christina also wanted everyone to have new beds in the bunkrooms because they were all worn out and uncomfortable.

Christina went to a clothing store and bought some beautiful dresses, then treated her crew to drinks at the tavern after she got all dressed up. They spent a few days in Tortuga picking up new members, and treating her crew to whatever they needed. By the time they left, the entire crew had new clothes.

They let the ones that refused to join free on Tortuga so they wouldn't be stranded. Christina also bought herself another sword, and a flintlock pistol.

They boarded the ship, plenty of food stocked and plenty of coins lining their pockets. Christina carried everything to the captain's cabin, still shocked at the beauty of the room,

Alex had it redone while they were there. The room was still the same size but the walls had a design painted on it in gold, with Prohibido Saqueo painted in some sort of Tribal design.

Alex walked in the room and leant against the doorway. “Do you like it, I have it painted on the outside of the ship in English for you. I figured new captain, new name.”

She trailed her fingers along the eloquent wording. “It’s beautiful but why would we name the ship after a treasure we already found?” She asked.

He walked up to her and took her lips in a daring kiss. “Because you will always be my forbidden plunder.” He answered as he took her hand.

PART 2

A CAPTAIN'S LIFE

CHAPTER 8

Christina dressed for the day, still in a haze from the night before. She put her breeches on followed by her usual dark corset. She walked on deck to do a head count then.

Oliver walked up to her, as if to have read her mind. "We lost Clarence through the night captain, which leaves us short by five men. How be Alex?"

"His fever is starting to go down, so whatever Xavier and Tyler did it's helping the infection greatly." Christina answered. She didn't really want to talk about what had happened aboard the ship the other day, because they almost lost.

Just the thought of it brought the memories swirling back into her mind, and all of a sudden she was back there again.

She had called war on the merchant ship that had been following them for weeks. They were running low on supplies and they needed food. The bastards let them board claiming they surrendered but as soon as they did they all fought back, and even a group came across the gangway to where she and Alex stood alone.

She tried her hardest to fight beside Alex and help but he took the first opportunity he had to throw her into the captain's cabin and locked her in there. She was pissed as she watched through the window yelling at him. As she tried to get out of the room she saw her crew being forced back over the gangway, she saw Philip get cut down, and the blood from his neck spewed up all over the window she was watching out of. She could feel her stomach churning and she knew she was about to vomit so she ran to the porthole and released her stomach contents. The tears streaming down her cheeks were uncontrollable.

She was horrified by what was happening and she wished she could be out there helping. She continued to ram into the door with her shoulder, but the second she got to where she could get out Oliver fixed it so she couldn't. She continued fighting the doorway until she saw that her crew was pushing the merchant men back. Finally, Tyler let her out of the Captain's cabin as the rest of the crew was taking the supplies from the merchant ship.

She looked around as the injured crew sat there, Alex was injured, the other surgeon was dead, and Xavier was moving as fast as he could to help Martin who was bleeding out on the floorboards of the ship.

Tyler walked up to her and handed her a hot piece of metal. "I'm going to hold him down, you need to burn his wounds." Tyler said as he ripped Alex's shirt open enough to see where the dagger had went into his shoulder.

He forced Alex to lay down. "You're going to need to sit on him. Quickly." He demanded.

She did. She would never forget the screams she had caused. All the pain aboard the ship. Martin had bled out before she could even finish cauterizing Alex's wound. She and Tyler had to run around doing this all day it seemed, even with Oliver helping Isaac.

It had been three days since then, and they were headed back to Tortuga by that night. Pete had died aboard the other ship, and George, the one they had just recruited had died throughout the second night. By the time she got finished taking care of the injured men, she realized why Alex locked her in the room this time. He had to have known the ship. She wanted to ask him about it, but he hadn't really been awake enough for her to. She was going to ask him as soon as he was awake enough to answer. Over the few days it had taken for them to get back to Tortuga Alex's fever was back to normal, and he was finally starting to come out of the sickness also.

Christina wondered what Tyler and Xavier did to help him, but it was working so she wasn't too worried about it. She knew Xavier's mother was some sort of medicine woman, and people often took her as a witch, so most of them feared her unless they needed her help.

She rushed the men in the crew to get back to Tortuga as fast as possible, they were short so many people that if someone declared battle on their ship they would surely lose everything they had fought the last year to get.

The last year of her life had been the best one yet and the worst one all the same, she had become the Captain of a wonderful crew, and even though that was the hardest thing she had ever done, the crew was like a family that she never had. She had fought beside them and saved their lives as much as they had saved hers. Yes this was definitely her home now, her heart belonged there as much as she did.

As they came up close to Tortuga she ordered the men to drop the anchor. She walked into the Captain's cabin almost shocked to see that Alex was dressing himself. He turned and smiled at her, causing her heart to leap into her throat. She was overcome by relief.

"Are ye gonna put on one of yer dresses, luv?" He asked.

"No, I'm gonna go like this." She answered as she grabbed her beautiful purple tricorned hat, with three peacock feathers pinned to the left side. She put it on her head, leaning it forward just enough to hide her eyes with the shadow.

Alex walked up to her, and pulled her close, taking her lips in a kiss filled with so much passion that it almost hurt. "I like ye better like this anyways, looks more like the woman I fell in love with."

Her cheeks flared red. "We should get going." She said quickly. "We need to find at least five more recruits."

"Did we lose that many?" He asked.

"Philip, Martin, Pete, George, and Clarence died just recently." She stated.

"Damn, I liked Philip."

"I liked all of them." She interrupted, tears starting to fill the corners of her eyes, thinking about everything she had lost aboard this ship, all the stuff that everyone else knew about, plus what she had kept hidden to herself. "I should have never called for war on that merchant ship." She added turning around.

"It wasn't your fault, you didn't know what was going to happen." Alex answered running his hands down her arms.

"But you did." She returned looking at him.

"How do ye know that?" He asked, obviously caught off guard by that statement.

"You've never locked me in the cabin when a battle broke out before, you knew the ship Alex." She answered.

"It was one of my father's merchant ships, one of the toughest of all the ships he owns, he paid for the strongest men to work on that ship, and I am honestly surprised that we made it out alive." Alex stated.

"Do you think they recognized you?" Christina asked.

"It didn't seem like it, but I could be wrong." He answered.

“What would happen if they did?” She asked, knowing what the answer was, but she had to hear it from him to be sure.

“Well, they would report to my father, and tell him the coordinates of where they had seen me and where they think I would be headed.” Alex answered.

“And then we’d have to fight him.” She interrupted.

“No, we’d have to run, he keeps so many guns and shot aboard his ship, and he hires people who really know their way around swords.” Alex returned.

“We should get going to Tortuga, we have loads of people to find, and I know the crew is wanting to relax.” She changed the subject quickly.

He nodded his agreement and followed her out of the Captain’s cabin.

CHAPTER 9

They sat at a table near the front of the tavern. Christina was watching all the people there and trying to see if there were any pirates she wanted to add to her ship. Before long a wench walked up to her.

"We aren't supposed to sit down with customers unless we are on their laps, and convincing them to pay for us." She said in a quiet, shy tone.

"I'm not a wench, I'm a captain." Christina answered, smiling. It wasn't the first time she had been confused for a wench, considering they were usually the only women that came into the taverns around here.

"Do you allow women aboard your ship?" The woman asked.

She nodded her head.

"What happens to them?"

"There is a part in the articles of agreement that no woman is to be harmed aboard my ship, unless it's for a reason in one of the other articles or from another ship during a raid, women are perfectly safe." Christina answered.

"Are you looking for people?" She asked.

"Yes, I need at least five people, but just because they are women they won't get special treatment, they'll have to work as hard as the rest of the crew." Christina answered. "What's yer name?"

"Alaina." She answered.

"Are you interested in coming aboard the Forbidden Plunder?" Christina asked.

"Yes and I know a couple of others that would be." Alaina answered.

"Well, you'd have to come to the ship and sign the articles of agreement, and so would the others." Christina stated.

"Can we meet here in an hour? I think I have four people besides me that would want to join." Alaina answered.

"We'll still be here by that time." Christina assured her.

The hour went by fast and before Christina could even realize it Alaina was walking up with a few well dressed women following close beside her. Alaina's dark brown hair was no longer up and practically hidden by the hat she was wearing, and the clothes she wore helped her amber eyes burst with color. She smiled at Christina.

"This is Chao-Ming." She started gesturing towards a small Asian woman with black hair and brown eyes. "This is Heather." She said gesturing towards the all too familiar redheaded wench that once seated herself among Alex's lap with Christina right there. "This is Mary." she added as she pointed towards the timid blonde girl that was half hidden behind Heather. "And this is Zendaya."

She finished pointing to the black woman with really curly black hair and light brown eyes.

Christina tried not to glare at Heather, she knew it was her job to flirt with the customers but she couldn't help but feel a jealousy, knowing that the woman would be on the ship with Alex all the time. She tried to swallow the feeling as she stood up. “Alright, let's go sign the articles and see who all wants to stay after wards.” Chris said as she tipped her tricornered hat down a little more then started out the door, heading towards the ship, not even bothering to look back and see if the women were still following her.

When they got to the ship she called the women in one by one, and sat there either while they read through the articles of agreement or she read them to the one's that couldn't read for themselves. Once they all signed the articles she made sure they knew that because they were women they would not be receiving special treatment of any kind, they would be expected to work just as hard as the men did. She informed them all to get all their stuff ready that they would be leaving in the morning. When she was done having them all sign the articles she called Alex in. She loomed over the look he gave Heather on her way out of the Captain's cabin.

“There isn't going to be a problem with the two of you is there?” She asked bluntly as she fiddled with the feather on the quill that everyone had used to sign the articles.

“No, at least not with me anyways.” He answered.

“I don't care if you are co-captain of this ship, no fighting aboard, and if you cheat on me, I will take something more precious than your life.” She added, not caring if she sounded insane or not.

His eyes widened and his mouth dropped. “Aye, Captain.” He answered before he could say something that would just make her angrier. He was bothered that she even though he would though, but he knew no matter what he said she would get mad, his only option was to agree.

She stood up and walked over to the porthole and looked out over the ships coming to port. Some of them looked familiar, but one stood out over the rest, the same ship that they had attacked that almost killed them all. Why would a merchant ship be in Tortuga though? She walked away from the porthole and turned to face Alex.

“Are we just going to stay on the ship tonight?” She asked.

“It'd probably be best, the men are out doing the ungodly things you hate, and Oliver is selling all the loot.” Alex answered.

“We could go back to the tavern.” She answered.

“We have all the crew members we need and I hate how the men always talk to you like yer a wench.” He answered.

“We could get a room at one of the Inns.” She answered.

“Why are you so worried about what to do all the time, take time to relax for once Christina.” Alex said.

“I relax all the time.” She returned.

“I haven't seen it fer almost a year now, yer always keeping yerself busy, ye can't stand to sit still.” Alex returned, raising his voice.

“I've killed people Alex, I have literally taken other peoples’ lives into my hands and either killed them myself or sent them to their deaths, do you think it would be easy to just relax after being the cause of such dear friends to see their ends, cause it's not.” She returned, turning away from him.

“Yer not the only one aboard this ship with blood on their hands, it be all of us, we are pirates, and you killed before you even came aboard.” He returned.

“That was to save myself, now I am doing it fer money.”

“We're doing it to survive, it takes money to survive Christina, and we all do it.”

She dismissed his statement, not wanting to argue over the matter anymore. She knew what she was getting into when she first signed the articles, she just didn't know it would be this hard to deal with. She felt Alex rub his warm hands down her arms, then kiss her cheek.

“Let's go to sleep luv, it's late and you want to be out of here, first thing in the morn.” He stated, trying to comfort her, at least a little.

"I'm not tired." She returned.

"Bullshit, Christina, you always say that. You have to get some decent sleep soon or yer gonna go mad from it." He yelled. "What is yer problem lately?"

"I already told you and I don't want to talk about it anymore." She returned as she stormed out of the captain's cabin. Angry that there were no more longboats left she dove straight into the water and swam to shore.

Alex shook his head. He honestly hated how she had been acting lately, she was always jealous, and was always upset over something petty. He had watched her closely up until the battle that he locked her away in. At first she was gaining weight, and then out of nowhere the weight went away, when she was getting plump she had a glow to her, he was sure that she was pregnant, but she never told him anything. He would still bet that she had lost the baby from malnutrition or one of the small battles that they had gotten into. However if she would have told him something he would have been able to console her. Now he felt like she didn't trust him.

He dove into the water with no worry about his wounds, and chased after her, knowing he was going to piss her off more when he asked her. He followed her through the town and pulled her into a dark alley. "Were you pregnant?" He asked.

"What does it matter?" She returned looking at the cobblestone rocks laid out.

“It does because that's obviously what is bothering you.” He answered. “Why didn't you tell me?”

“I lost it before I even knew.” She stated, trying not to let the tears surface at the thought of what could have been.

“If you would have told me we could have talked about it, instead of you acting like a jealous lunatic.”

“If you think I am a lunatic why the hell are you chasing after me.” She yelled as she shoved the palm of her hand into his chest, pushing him away.

She walked away, not even checking to see if he was alright. She felt bad hearing him gasp for air, but he shouldn't have said that. He came up behind her and grabbed her throwing her against the wall of the grungy building they were next to.

“Why is it so hard for you to talk about this with me, we both lost a child and you want to walk away from it as if it didn't matter, like you do everything else.” He yelled. Looking at the tears that were now streaming down her face the answer became crystal clear. “You wanted it.” His heart practically stopped at his statement. “You wanted it so bad that you were going to quit.”

She turned her head. Everything he had said was true. She was going to leave and raise the baby, by herself if she had to, but then she lost the baby before they could even make it to land and the thought was just thrown out. She tried to forget about it but it seemed that it just festered inside of her.

She leaned her head into Alex's strong muscular chest, knowing she couldn't get away this time without seriously hurting him. She cried as he wrapped his arms around her shoulders, feeling the comfort of it seemed to make it feel like she could breakdown and actually cry for the first time since it happened a couple of months ago.

Alex felt bad, because he had his hunches about what was going on but he refused to believe it because he was sure she would have told him. There were so many signs though he should have known instead of letting her deal with it all alone. He felt terrible and guilty, he kissed her forehead. “I'm sorry, I should have known something was wrong.”

“So much has been going on since then, it wasn't really the first priority.” She answered.

He lifted her chin with his finger. “You are always my first priority.” He said, then kissed her lips lovingly. “I love you, me amour.”

“I love you too.” she answered.

He started walking her towards the nearest inn and paid for a room. He got her up to the room and in bed. He wasn't sure what to do so he just laid next to her, patiently waiting for the sun to start coming up. He had been sleeping so much since his injury it was impossible for him to fall asleep.

When Christina woke, Alex was sitting on the bed next to her, facing the window just staring out at the harbor. She put her hand on his back. “Are you alright?” She asked.

“Yes.” He answered quickly. “Did you notice the ship that has been following us?” He asked.

“Yes, but I didn't think much of it, I figured we were just headed to the same place.” She answered.

“It makes no sense though, I've seen the same ship since shortly after the secret island with the forbidden plunder treasure on it. Why would they keep following us? It's not a pirate ship, and merchant ships don't usually come to Tortuga, unless they desperately need supplies and I've seen that ship here every time we have come here.”

“Are you sure it's the same ship?” Christina asked as she stood up and walked over to the window.

“Yes, I am also sure that it is the same one from the attack.” Alex returned.

“That's ridiculous, they have no reason to be following us.” Christina answered. “We are already running late we should get to the ship and get headed to Barbados.”

“Why are we going to Barbados, I thought you never wanted to go back there?” He asked.

“It's been over a year, I am pretty sure that I am safe to go back there for now, it's either that or we head to Veracruz.” She returned.

“Why there?” He asked.

"I have my reasons for wanting to go back to Barbados, and I know you have been thinking about going back to Veracruz, I just don't know why you want to go back. I figure if we go back for a little while, just to tie up loose ends then we can forget about those places and work on taking over the high seas." She said as she placed her hat on top of her head. She walked over to Alex and kissed him confidently.

He smiled and followed her out of the inn. He kept his hands in his pockets as they continued to walk, glad to see her close to her usual self for the first time in months. He wasn't shocked when they got to the harbor when they saw the last half of the crew climbing into the last longboat, they hollered and ran to them, barely getting there in time to catch them. As soon as Christina got aboard the ship she started introducing the new members to the old ones.

She started commanding the crew, in more detail than usual for the new members to get the ship ready and on its way to Barbados. Everyone aboard the ship that had been there for a while was shocked when she said to head to Barbados. Some of them questioned it, but the only one that argued it was Tyler.

"Uhh... Captain, why Barbados, I don't think we should go there." Tyler said.

"Because I said Barbados." She returned, a stern look on her face.

"What if they recognize you?" He asked.

"Then I will suffer the consequences, or you'll have to break me out like pirates do." She returned as she walked up to the quarterdeck and overlooked the crew hustling and bustling to get the boat on track.

"Christina, there is no reason for us to go there."

"Yes there is." She answered quickly.

"Do you have a death wish?" Tyler returned, raising his voice so loud that Henry was startled.

"It's none of your business Tyler, get back to work." She demanded pointing down towards the other crew members.

"It is my job to protect you and Alex, remember? I am the Bosun that is my job and I think what you are doing is foolish." He answered.

"I have a good reason, just leave it alone, I will tell you later." She said, her teeth gritted together.

He glared for a minute, then just walked down the stairs to the deck and began helping them drop the sails. Christina walked down the stairs shortly after and started to help the men raise the anchor. She quickly got lost in the work and smell of the fresh ocean water. The time just seemed to fly by and she started to succumb to the peace of the waves underneath the hull. This was definitely where she belonged in this world, but she had to go back and get the book that her mother had left her.

She wouldn't have worried much about it but the book that her mother had left for her was the one her father had written, and left before he disappeared. She remembered that the book was written while he was on a merchant ship headed to Veracruz to transfer some goods over, and she was sure it was to the Boseuilla family, she was sure it was about Alex's father. That was the only reason she wanted it, because it listed all the Boseuilla ships and she knew Alex was worried about the merchant ship that had been following them.

She knew that they were following her, but she wasn't sure if they knew that it was Alejandro's son that was aboard this ship, and she had a feeling that they knew that Alex wouldn't just climb on their ship and be taken back to his parents. She was aware that if they tried to fight with them again she would lose even more of her crew, which was another reason she wanted to go to Barbados, she knew someone that would be more than happy to join the crew and he was strong enough to help them.

They all needed to lay low until they could get there though. She watched as the crew finished up all their work, then she told the new members to swab the deck, with how many there was it didn't take much longer than a couple of hours for them to finish. When they finished she watched Heather as she walked over to Alex and they started talking. She couldn't help but feel angry at both of them. She had to fight her urges to go over there and pull her away from him. She was thankful when Tyler and Oliver walked up to her.

"Miss, I do believe we need to have a discussion, downstairs in the chart room with Henry." Oliver stated.

"Mum, yes we do." She answered as she continued to stare at Alex and Heather out of her peripheral vision as they walked down to the barracks.

She barely got to close the door to the chart room before Henry started in on her. "We have time to change our course, Captain."

"We have no need to change our course." She answered. "If you all haven't noticed we have had a ship following us for a couple of months now, we go to Barbados."

"Why, you're risking your life over a ship following us." Tyler interrupted.

"No, I am risking my life over a Spanish ship that is following us, also the same ship that killed half of my crew, and the same ship that might be trying to break my crew up again." She answered.

"What do you mean?" Oliver asked.

"Alex believes that the ship is one of his father's and I think they might be trying to take him back to his parents. " She started. "Back in Barbados I have a book that my father had written describing all of the Boseuilla ships and crew members from when he was working for Alejandro. I need that book so we can know the weak spots on the ship and I also need to contact a friend of mine that might be able to help, because if we are right, they will attack again and try to kill us all. So I am risking my life for the entire crew's well-being, which is more than enough for me."

"Well, if you're sure about this, I will come to land with you so that I can try to protect you, but the smaller the numbers is better so we won't get noticed." Tyler stated.

"We have at least a week, depending on the ocean's mood." She said. "We'll have time to figure out what we are going to do, but I want to keep this quiet from the crew so there won't be a panic, and I also don't want Alex to know, because there is a chance that they haven't recognized him yet."

They nodded their heads and she walked out of the chart room and up to the quarterdeck, irritated that Alex and Heather were still standing there, talking as if they were the best of friends. "You." She said pointing. "Why don't you go make yourself useful in the galley, I'm sure Hugh will be grateful for the help."

Heather gave her a quick glare then folded her arms over her overly large breasts and started walking downstairs to the galley. Alex's lip quirked up on one side as he shook his head. He knew as well as she did that she didn't want him talking to Heather. He would have to ask her about it later though, since he didn't want to make a scene in front of the crew, especially with the new members all there, except for Heather. He had never really seen Christina get jealous, but it was oddly arousing.

CHAPTER 10

Alex walked into the room well after Christina, making sure that everything was secured for the night first. He wasn't shocked to see her just sitting in the bed. He smiled at her but she didn't smile in return.

"What's going on with you and Heather?" She demanded.

"Absolutely nothing, me amour." He answered as he pulled his shirt off.

"It didn't look like nothing." She returned.

He crawled on top of the bed so he was hovering over her, kissing her neck as he went along. He pushed her beautiful dark hair away from the bare skin on her shoulder. "You know you're the only woman that I want." He whispered sultrily, kissing her lips tenderly.

She returned his kiss almost forgetting about what they were talking about as he started to pull the laces of her corset free. She missed the feeling of his fingers trailing her bare skin and it was welcomed as he did it. She could feel the heat rise as more and more of their clothing was removed, until she was completely embraced by his warmth. She could feel the tide rolling, inside and out when he started, then nothing but warm waves crashing around her as she reached her peak. She remembered then, exactly why she had loved him for so long, he knew her better than she knew herself. He was so in tune with her mind and her body that it was always so intense no matter what they were doing.

When he rolled off of her she smiled and kissed his lips. "I miss the way you make me feel." She whispered.

"I've missed it too." He returned, smiling brightly as he panted to catch his breath.

"I'm sorry I've been such a wreck lately." She said.

"I understand, and I've been no better." He answered. "And I'll stop talking to Heather if that is what you want."

"No, I think it was just that it's been so long since we have actually been together, alone. We're always with the crew or out trying to get more people for the crew, we never have time for just ourselves." She returned. "Maybe after we go to Barbados, we'll just find a place to take a nice long vacation at. Get maybe a month away from everything and just relax."

"That sounds great, me amour, but where would we go?" He questioned.

Moving her head to where it was resting on his bare chest, "We'll just follow the horizon and see where it leads." She said as she closed her eyes, allowing herself to fall into the usual comfort the sound of his heartbeat brought her. It was like a white noise, bringing her to her deep slumber.

When she awoke she felt completely rejuvenated. She got up and dressed herself, kissing Alex before she walked out on deck, she wasn't surprised that the crew had already been on top of pulling the sails down and getting the ship up to full speed. She was grateful that she had a good crew. She walked down to the galley and checked to make sure that Heather was still down there helping Hugh.

Walking back up on deck she enjoyed the feel of the breeze running through her hair and the smell of the ocean tickling her nose as if it was all brand new to her. It was like it was her first day at sea again, but even better. She definitely loved the adventure and the people that she had met. She would never look back from this life, nor would she ever want to.

The rest of the voyage to Barbados was the same, everything seemed so much better than it had been. She and Alex were finally rekindling their relationship, while the crew seemed to be even closer than usual. However that ship still followed, keeping more distance than they had been. She had no idea what they were planning but she always felt like she was being watched. She noticed that Alex kept glancing over his shoulder too, and a lot of the crew members also.

As soon as they made port Christina and Tyler got off the ship, unnoticed by the busy crew, leaving Oliver to explain to Alex what was going on if they didn't get back before Oliver and Alex did. It was planned perfectly, Christina and Tyler had Oliver ask Alex to help him with the loot, they left as soon as Alex and Oliver was out of sight. They weren't going to stay there longer than they needed so they were trying to hurry before Christina could be recognized.

As she made her way to her old master's house she felt overwhelmed with guilt. Her stomach started tossing and turning. Seeing the abandoned house falling apart as if it hadn't been taken care of since she left, she realized how many people she put out of work, just by killing that one man. She could feel the sting in her eyes, the burning telling her she was going to cry. She wiped her eyes roughly to try and stop the tears. She walked up and turned the doorknob almost shocked that it wasn't rusted.

She made her way down to the lowest level of the house where her room had been and started searching through her dusty, gross, and rusted belongings until she found the fabric that the book was wrapped in. She unwrapped it, hoping the book itself wasn't as moldy as the fabric, and was relieved to see that the damage wasn't that bad.

Christina and Tyler hurried out of the house and to the blacksmith she needed to see, who amazingly was still right next to the harbor. She barged through the door, almost shocked to see that he was standing there, wiping clean one of his blades. He looked up from his work and dropped the sword, barely catching it before it could hit the wooden floorboards of the shop.

"Christina?" He said, his voice was still hoarse and deep, as he was still burly and large.

"James." She returned with a smile.

"You sure are a sight for sore eyes." He said as he walked up to her, setting the sword he was working on the counter as he passed by it, surely enough to clear his hands so he could show her his affection. As he laid a kiss on her cheek awfully close to her lips she tugged herself out of his arms.

"I am sorry James, I am here strictly for business." She said.

"Well what is it that a lovely lady like you can use from a blacksmith like me?" He asked.

"I need a blacksmith." She returned.

"Well what do you need from me, you've disappeared for over a year and now you come here to tell me that you need a blacksmith, what is going on Christina?" James asked.

"I am the captain of a pirate ship now and we are being followed by a dangerous foe, I know you are very good with a sword, along with being able to make them and repair them. I need you aboard my ship." She was blunt.

"And what do I get out of moving all my stuff onto your ship and packing up and leaving my shop, I am very successful here, and it has become obvious that you have no interest in me anymore." He started.

She dropped a bag of gold coins into his large calloused hands. He ran his free hand through his long, unkempt dark hair and smiled. "This is almost as much as I make in a month." He stated.

"You'll also get a cut of all the profits we make aboard the ship until you decide to leave." She added.

"I'll need help getting all me stuff aboard." He answered.

"We'll take you back to the ship and you can pick out a few men to come and help." She stated as she walked out of the house, knowing that James and Tyler were following close behind her. She was careful to watch for guards and sneak around them. She knew they were looking for her so the quicker they got back to the ship the better. It didn't take them long to get to the harbor, then to the ship.

Alex ran up to her as soon as she boarded. "What the hell Christina are you trying to get yourself hung?" His voice was stern.

"Not at all." She returned with a smile.

"Then why did you go?" He asked.

No sooner than he got the words out of his mouth, James and Tyler were boarding the ship. Alex didn't say much else. He shook his head and walked into the captain's cabin. He came back out with the book that the articles of agreement were in, rolling his eyes at Christina as he walked passed her.

She knew he was upset with her, but he read the articles to James quickly and James signed it. He picked out a few people to go with him, including Alex and Tyler. Henry argued about going, but Christina ordered him to go and he nodded his agreement. It took them about an hour and a half to get his supplies then they left Barbados, staying up until they were out of reach for the royal navy to take them down.

Christina was hoping she would get to sneak off to the Captain's quarter without any argument but she was not so lucky. As soon as she turned to walk in Alex stopped her. “Why the hell didn't you send someone else?” He asked, his voice raised enough for the crew members still on deck to hear.

“Nobody else knows James.” She answered.

“So you could have sent someone to retrieve him.” Alex returned.

“He is a person not an item.”

“And you could have been hung.”

“I am the captain of this ship and it is my duty to do what is best for this crew, even if it means putting my life on the line. This is what you wished for when we led the mutiny against Billy. I will not put my crew's life before my own and we need James, and a blacksmith aboard the ship gives us an obvious advantage.” Her voice was raised, her eyes showed the fierceness in her heart at those words.

“You could have taken protection.” Alex returned, lowering his voice.

“I had Tyler with me. It is his job to protect me is it not?” She stated.

“You could have taken more people.” He said.

“Two people wondering through the streets is less suspicious than three or four, this was well planned out.” She said.

“Then why wasn't I told about it?” He asked.

“Because you would have stopped me.” She answered. “Now, I am going to sleep, what's done is done and there is no reason to argue about it.” She turned and walked through the door, shutting it before he could say anything else.

She was almost glad that he didn't come to bed right then, she was angry that he always had to yell at her as if she was a child, but she was tired of fighting. He knew exactly what they were getting into when they started planning the mutiny but he still had to argue all of her choices. She closed her eyes as soon as she heard the door start creaking open hoping that he hadn't realized that she was still awake. He just laid down on the other side of the bed, not saying one word, and barely even covering himself up with the blanket that they shared.

CHAPTER 11

When Alex awoke Christina was no longer in the room with him. He knew that was going to happen but he hoped it wouldn't, he wanted to talk to her alone, but he knew she was angry with him. However, he had every right to be concerned. He walked out on deck squinting his eyes from the brightness until his eyes could adjust then continued to look around, seeking out Christina, but unable to spot her before Heather could come up to him.

"So I see that you and the Captain are fighting again." She started, her tone of voice was sultry as if she was picking at him to see what she could get from him.

"Ye heard that?" He asked.

"Aye, I believe the entire ship did. I and the girls heard it from in our bunk room. I was surprised that you didn't come down to accompany me for the night." She added as she ran her hand down his chest till she reached his abdomen.

"Ye know that's not going to happen." Alex said as he grabbed her wrist and made her stop.

"You know you used to look at me the way you look at her, we can always go back to that. She can't kick you off the ship for breaking up with her." Heather stated.

“I love her Heather, and I'm not ruining that.” He stated.

She pulled her hand away. “I don't see how she is better than I am to you.” She yelled then walked away quickly. Alex ignored her as he continued looking around for Christina, when he found her talking to Henry up at the capstan on the quarterdeck he walked up there slowly. He smiled when she excused herself from Henry.

“Yes, Alex, I am very busy.” She said as she walked down from the quarterdeck.

“I understand that as captain there are things you must do to protect your crew instead of yourself, but why was this one man so important?” He asked.

“He's a blacksmith, and I know he is great with a sword, we could really use him to avoid another outcome like the last battle.” She said.

“Are you sure that's all?” He asked.

“Yes Alex, that's all, you have no room to feel jealous considering that your favored wench is now aboard my ship swooning over you constantly.” She returned.

“So basically you risked your life because you're jealous?” He questioned.

“No, I risked my life because I had to, if you would rather have that harlot go for it I don't care.” She returned and walked down to the barracks.

He hated it when she walked away, but he was so furious at what she said he followed her down the stairs and to the chart room. He didn't care that Henry and Oliver were standing there when he grabbed her arm and made her listen.

"If I wanted her so bad why wouldn't I have taken her?" his voice was louder than he intended.

"I'm busy Alex." She returned, not even looking away from the map she was looking over.

"Not too busy to throw accusations in my face then walk away as if nothing ever happened." He yelled.

"You accused me first, Alex. I'm not jealous of some whore that is only in love with the thought of money." She answered, raising her voice louder than his. "I am busy we will discuss this later." She added gesturing to the door.

Alex walked out, angry that she was still trying to act like nothing was going on. He knew something was going on with her and James. He could tell it by the way James stared at her every chance he got. Seeing him just standing on deck, staring at the stairs down to the barracks infuriated him even more. He charged up to him.

"What the hell is your interest in my woman?" Alex yelled, with his hand on the hilt of his sword, ready to fight.

"Christina is a close friend of mine." James answered, not even looking at Alex.

"I see the way you look at her, and I don't like it one bit." Alex said, teeth clenched along with his fists.

"What do ye expect, mate, ye've got the best piece of arse aboard this damn ship." James returned, not caring if he offended Alex or not.

Alex went to swing at James, not caring that he was a much larger size than he was, but he was quickly stopped by Tyler pulling him away from him and restraining his arms. "Calm down Alex." He said as Alex struggled to get his arms free.

Tyler drug him into the Captain's cabin and kicked the door shut, shoving Alex forward and standing in front of the door so he couldn't make a run for it.

"I'll let you calm down before you start explaining to me what that little mess was about." Tyler said as he crossed his arms over his chest.

Alex took a deep breath. "I know there is something going on between him and Christina."

"Other than the fact that he tried to kiss her and she pulled away quicker than she would have if it was a burning hot piece of steel." Tyler returned. "She won't let anything happen."

"You see the way he looks at her." Alex stated.

"And you still haven't claimed her permanently Alex, if you're so worried about her leaving you, don't you think there is something you should be asking her, something you have been talking about for a while now." The question was rhetorical.

"She thinks I am cheating on her with Heather." Alex returned.

"So, show her that you're not." Tyler's answers sounded so simple compared to the task he was speaking of.

"How am I supposed to do that?" Alex asked.

"Show her that you only have eyes for her, and quit acting like a jealous imbecile." Tyler answered.

He pushed his ear against the door then, hearing Christina yelling as she walked on to the deck of the ship. He chuckled as he heard her scream, "Where the hell is that arse?"

"Maybe wait until she isn't so angry at you." Tyler said as he stepped away from the door. "Sorry mate." He added opening the door and rushing out before Christina could walk in the room.

When Christina walked into the room Alex went ahead and stood up to close the door but Christina stopped him. "Why are you so worried about privacy now, you didn't seem to care when you barged downstairs and started yelling, why the hell should you care now, they have already heard all of it."

"I was angry Christina and wasn't thinking, these are private matters." He tried not to raise his voice.

“So accusing me of being a Harlot isn't.” She returned.

His eyes widened and his heart shattered. He felt like a total arse for saying those awful things. He shook his head and tried to shut the door again, but she caught it and stopped it from shutting.

“I apologize Christina.” He said.

“Louder, come on since the crew needs to hear everything about our lives and your silly accusations.” She demanded.

“I'm sorry, Christina, I was wrong, and I should have never said those things about you, now please shut the door.” He requested.

She let it shut, seeing that he truly did feel bad. “Now what has come over you?” She asked, calmly.

“I don't know, just you risked your life to bring back one man, Christina, and I never want to lose you over anything.” He said as he ran the side of his hand along her cheek, he kissed her lips lovingly. “I want to marry you Christina.” He finally admitted.

She was left speechless, her head started spinning just like her stomach. She felt the need to vomit but she forced it away.

“Just say yes, please just say that you want to marry me too.” Alex pleaded as he took her hand in his.

“Yes I do, but is now the best time to decide, we've been fighting all day.” She answered.

“I'm not saying we get married today. I just want to know today.” Alex returned.

“Then yes.” She answered, slightly hesitant. “But this whole jealousy thing has to stop.”

“Alright.” He answered smiling as he walked over to the desk and opened the drawer. He walked back over to her and placed the small silver ring on her finger.

“I'll get you a better one when we get to land.” He said.

She looked it over. The silver band complimented the diamond and seemed to make it shine even more with the twisted design on the band. “This one is perfect.” She said and kissed his lips, unable to stop the stray tear that slid down her cheek. She wiped her face. “We should get back to work.” She added with a smile, kissing him one more time before she walked out the door.

Alex took a deep breath, feeling like he had been holding it in the entire time they were talking. He felt restless then to get back to land and marry her. This was exactly what he had wanted his entire life was to marry a woman he loved, and even though she drove him mad he loved her more than life itself. Taking a few minutes to catch his breath before he walked back out on deck he went back to work.

CHAPTER 12

The next few days just seemed to fly by almost as fast as the wind swayed the sails. Christina was a lot happier, but she was nowhere near as happy as Alex was. Alex felt as if he had been walking on water for the last few days, even though they hadn't told anyone about the engagement yet he could feel the change aboard the ship.

Christina and him hadn't fought or even argued since then. The only one that had even bothered to question him about it was Tyler, but Alex would just smile and say that the crew heard it. He knew that Tyler would be the first he would tell about it but truth be told they didn't have much time to sit around and chit chat over stuff.

Alex had been keeping an eye out for that Spanish ship that had been following them and after three days of not seeing them he spotted them the first time that morning. He wasn't as worried about it since Christina had been reading the book her father wrote about the Boseuilla ships.

Alex knew a lot about them too but he had never actually been on the ships with the crew other than when he ran away from home, so he really had no idea what they were in for, until they found that book.

Christina's father described the weapons and all the members aboard the ship, how they fought and all their battle tactics, it was almost like he was planning on trying to take over the ship, but he was grateful for the details now, considering he was sure it was his father trying to get him back home.

Alex stared at the ship that was barely in sight, but it was still there, and he was sure that they were watching him. The ship wasn't much smaller than the Forbidden Plunder, like all of his father's ships it had a darker color of wood than most, his father always said the more expensive the wood the better it held up, and the dark cedar wood was some of the most expensive. Alex didn't really see the difference, other than the color, the ships didn't move faster and they were just as sturdy as all the other ships, no better no worse. Alex was sure his father did it just to flaunt his money around.

Tyler walked up to him then breaking him from his thoughts as he handed him a glass of rum. Alex took a sip, then looked away from the Spanish ship.

"So ye ready to tell me what happened?" Tyler asked.

"She said yes." He answered, smiling.

"You asked her?" Tyler returned, giving Alex a surprised look. "While she was that pissed off at you."

"She wasn't that mad after I apologized, just wished she would have calmed down before she made me apologize in front of the whole crew." Alex returned.

"She wasn't in the wrong there, she could have done a lot worse than that, I am honestly surprised that was all she did, you pretty much said she was a whore, so loud that everyone could hear it." Tyler returned.

"Aye, I know I should have used me head a bit more, but what can I do now?" Alex said.

"At least it all has been calmed down for a while." Tyler said, making the motion of a man tying a noose around his neck.

"Yeah it did get really bad there for a while." Alex answered.

"It wasn't even just her, you were being an arse too. Now what is it out there you keep staring at?" Tyler asked looking out over the ocean.

"That damn ship is back." Alex answered.

"I don't know why you two are so worried about that ship, it might not be the same one that almost killed you." Tyler returned.

"No, it is, it's my father's ship I am sure about that." Alex stated.

"Speaking of father's has Christina told you anything about what happened to hers?" Tyler asked, not wanting to listen to him talk about the ship following them anymore.

"No, you know she doesn't talk about her family, all I know is that her mother sold her as a servant." Alex answered.

"That's harsh." Tyler returned. "I understand making her work, but selling her as a servant, no wonder she doesn't talk much about her family."

"Tyler, I'm worried that my father is going to try to do something worse than make me go back." Alex said, finally getting the weight off his chest a little by confiding in his closest friend.

"What do you mean?" Tyler asked.

"My father is more conniving than to just force me back home. I am sure that he's got something bigger planned." Alex started. "I'm worried that he's not going to come after just me, if he comes after me at all. My father is known for being very manipulative, he is a world known trader, and usually gets really great deals on everything he buys and trades, making more of a profit than a lot of people, I have a feeling he's going to try and manipulate me to come back, no matter what it takes."

"So basically you're worried about Christina." Tyler stated.

Alex nodded then swallowed the last of the rum in his glass. "I'm headed to bed for the night." He said then walked into the captain's cabin.

CHAPTER 13

When Alex awoke he was given direct orders to go down to the hold and start training the women to use the swords that James had given them. He wasn't too happy about being stuck down there with the women and James to watch over him, but at least he didn't have to worry about what James was doing while he was down there. He also had his suspicions about why Christina had sent James down there with them.

As he explained to the women how to hold their swords for the best stability, James would demonstrate how. The day continued on like that until the women had it down. He had to go around a few times and fix their stances or their grip.

He hated every time he had to help Heather with her swings, she would always make sure to rub her arse against him, even more than some of the other women were. By the time they got their swings down, Alex felt hot and had to rush away from the training to get himself calmed down, but as soon as he walked on deck Christina walked up to him.

"Are you done training them already?" She asked, her voice was as heated as he was, her smile was just as suggestive.

He almost choked on his own saliva when Heather walked up the stairs. "Yes we are done for the night, luv." He answered, wiping his forehead.

Christina looked over toward the stairs and saw Heather staring at Alex. She shook her head and walked away from him, rushing into the captain's cabin before he could stop her, but he followed anyway.

He beat on the door until she unlocked it. "Christina, what is wrong?" He asked, hoping she didn't notice.

"You think I can't tell when you're aroused?" She questioned, keeping her voice quiet instead of yelling.

"Nothing happened Christina." He returned.

"I don't care, you obviously want it to." She returned. "Do whatever you like."

He pushed his way into the room and shut the door behind him, slyly locking the door before he grabbed her and pulled her into him, sliding his hand down the back of her trousers until he reached her firm, round arse. He picked her up and shoved her against the door, placing himself between her thighs. He kissed her neck.

"Christina, you're the only one I want, ever." He stated.

As his lips trailed the soft skin on her neck she fell silent, all but the soft moans making their way passed her lips. Before he could finish his act of passion a call came out from the crow's nest. "Enemy ship approaching!"

The call was loud and rang through the captain's cabin just before the smash of a cannon hit the hull ripping through the wooden boards, but not enough to cause a severe leak.

He set her down and rushed out the door. "Batten down the hatches and prepare for battle." He yelled, extremely relieved to see that it wasn't the merchant ship that had been trailing them. He pulled his sword and held it in the air. "Dead men tell no tales."

Alex was a bit worried about the new recruits so he stayed as close to them as possible, while keeping some distance. He steadied himself as either Henry or Oliver shot their cannons in return. He glanced around the ship as they crashed into the broadside of the enemy ship, all men were in their places and wielding their swords at the ready. Oliver stood at the capstan, steering the ship into the other as another of their cannons shot, ripping through the other ship's hull, a huge hole appeared where the cannon ball had hit. He was shocked at how easily the other ship was coming apart.

He waited for the other ship to make its next move before he ordered anything to happen, but they started to run. "Alright let's go send these bastards to Davy Jones locker." He commanded.

"Leave 'em be, those poor bilge rats picked a battle they couldn't win and realized it. They were probably just low on supplies." Christina argued. "We have more important things to worry about right now."

Henry followed Christina's orders. Alex was shocked that she agreed to let someone go after attacking the ship. She never did that. He watched her as she grabbed Henry's spyglass and walked to the edge of the ship, watching the ship that had just attacked them. About an hour later, he saw what she was worried about.

The ship that just attacked them was stopped beside the ship that had been following them. He understood now, but how did she know that the two ships were working together. He watched her as she quietly spoke to Henry, then came down the stairs from the quarterdeck.

"How did you know that was one of my father's ships?" He asked quietly.

"I didn't, but I saw the two ships together in Barbados, and both Captains were talking, I didn't want to risk it." She answered.

She walked away before he could even answer. He continued watching the two ships as they moved away from them. He hoped that they were able to get far enough away from the ships that they didn't have to worry about them for a while.

They got pretty far away from the ships by night, but he was still worried about it by the time the crew started to head to the bunk rooms so he stayed up late. He was worried that something might happen to Christina if the ships did catch up to them. His father was a business man, and if any of the men aboard the Boseuilla ships saw him with Christina his father would know that it would be more beneficial to him to take her.

He hated having to worry about her like this. He honestly wished that he had been smarter and faked his death, but he just left. Now because of his ignorance, Christina and the entire crew was in danger, they had already lost so many people over him that he was honestly thinking about just going back so that the others wouldn't be harmed. He was overcome with guilt, and had been since the fight when they lost so many of their loyal crew members, but he dared not to tell Christina.

He stared at her and Tyler as they spoke to each other. He knew she had been talking to Tyler about the ship that had been following them for some time now, but they had never stayed up late like they were. He knew they were just as concerned as he was by their actions. They stayed out on deck most of the night, but Alex followed Christina into the captain's cabin as soon as she was ready. He was afraid to leave her out on deck alone.

She laid on the bed and he pulled her against him, holding her close until her breathing slowed, assuring him that she was asleep. He rejected the idea of loosening his hold on her, even though he knew it would be impossible for the other ships to approach unheard.

CHAPTER 14

Alex woke in a panic after the dream he had. All he could think about was Christina being pulled out of his arms, and he was completely helpless. It was even worse when woke and she wasn't in bed with him anymore. He jumped up and dressed himself, rushing out on the deck of the ship to find her.

Seeing her standing up on the quarterdeck with Oliver, his heartbeat calmed to normal as did his breathing. Glancing over the rails of the ship, the following ships were no longer in view. He knew that wasn't going to last long, and from his dreams alone he knew that something was going to happen soon. He swallowed his pride and walked over to James.

"You love her too, don't ye?" He stated, trying to keep himself under control.

"I don't know, I did at one time, but she doesn't feel that way about me anymore. Ye gonna get mad and try to fight me again?" James returned.

"No, I want to ask you for help." Alex answered.

"You want my help." James chuckled, knowing the extreme discontent that Alex had towards him.

"Aye, can we speak somewhere more private?" Alex asked.

James nodded, keeping his arms crossed. He started walking down into the barracks and into the room where all of his blacksmith equipment was. "What's this about?"

"Look, I know ye don't like me, and I don't much like ye either, but if ye loved Christina you'll understand." Alex started. "That ship that has been following us, I am sure it is one of my father's ships, and I am worried that they are out to harm Christina to get back at me and force me to return home. I know they are going to attack again, and I am sure they will try to take Christina."

"So ye want me to look after her." James stated.

"Aye, they know what she means to me, I am sure they have been watching. So I am sure when they attack they will be more focused on keeping me away from her, than anyone else." Alex returned.

"I'll do it, but I ain't doing it fer you either. I do love her, but I would never take another man's woman, and I don't like the way ye've been yelling at her. But I can tell she loves ya in a way she could never love me." James stated.

"Thank you." Alex said, feeling some relief in knowing that there would be someone else to keep her safe.

James grunted and walked back out of the room. Alex followed shortly after, ignoring Heather whom had tried to stop him from returning on deck. Christina walked up to him shortly after he got back up on deck.

"What's going on?" She asked.

"Nothing, just had a little chat with James, and we've come to an understanding." Alex stated then walked away, back to the perch he'd been keeping near the railings of the ship so he could easily see what was happening.

The smaller ship that had attacked them was barely viewable but the other was nowhere in sight, however he still knew it was close by. After hours of watching for the ship, he decided it was time to find something to do.

Alex walked around the ship, checking everything he walked by, trying not to glance over his shoulder. He started to wonder if he was just being paranoid, and considering how he had been acting lately, he wondered if he should stop worrying.

Christina had pretty much everything under control, she planned for another attack by that ship and he knew she would make the right choices if it came down to it. He found relief in knowing how she would give up everything to keep the crew safe, yet that was his biggest dilemma too.

Alex would rather keep Christina alive than anyone else. He loved her more than he loved life itself. He sat down on the stairs leading up to the quarterdeck and watched as the deck was tarred.

CHAPTER 15

Alex spent most the week in the captain's cabin, working on the map he requested Henry to make a copy of marking all the places where the two ships had followed them. He knew he was obsessing but he just kept at it. He also kept looking over the book Christina had gotten on the Boseuilla ships her father had worked on. He was making notes on the fighting tactics that were written down in there.

He also found a detailed description of where all the cannons were placed. At this point he was ready for whatever it was that they had planned.

He started copying all of his notes over, startled when Christina barged through the door. He hadn't realized how long it had been since he paid any attention to her until then.

She stood there, hands on her luscious curvy hips, tapping her foot on the floorboards as he looked up from the papers. She raised an eyebrow as he looked her up and down.

"Still busy?" She asked.

"Yes, but I'm almost finished." He stated as he stood up from the desk he had condemned himself to.

"What are you doing that is so important?" She asked as she walked over to the desk, leaning over the papers and books that were sprawled out.

He walked around to the side of the desk she was on, running his fingertips down her hips. He made her turn to face him and pushed her up so she was sitting on the desk, taking her lips in a deep, revitalizing kiss, almost taking the very breath she was breathing.

Christina ran her fingernails along the stubble on his neck, taken by surprise, she wrapped her legs around his waist, realizing just how much she had missed his company. She didn't fight as the passion itself took over, making their way from the desk to the bedroom.

Everything that once seemed so important, no longer did as their love for each other took over with the fiery passion that seemed to be lost to them. The waves crashing against the ship no longer mattered, and for the first time in a long time it was just the two of them that mattered.

When Alex awoke Christina was sitting up, barely covered by the blanket she was holding tightly against her chest. He heard a loud boom ring out in the night, was this what they had been preparing for? He had a sudden realization that he and Christina were still undressed. He threw her the clothes he had practically torn off of her last night and dressed quickly.

Grabbing all of his weapons he ran out on the deck of the ship, seeing every crewmember at the ready. Tyler stood by the railings, his sword out and ready. Alex walked up to him. "Who is it?" He questioned.

"It's your father's ship." Tyler answered.

Alex's eyes widened and his heartbeat quickened. "Lock Christina in the captain's cabin." He demanded.

"She'll be pissed, and she will get out." Tyler returned.

"Do it now!" Alex's voice was raised, he was determined to keep Christina safe as the Boseuilla ship came around one side, and the merchant ship around the other.

He glared at Tyler until he had the door secured shut. He felt guilty as he heard Christina pounding at the door and screaming at the top of her lungs, but she would thank him for it later. Men from the other ships started setting down gangways so they could board his ship and others swung over on ropes, he started swinging at each and every one of them that came into his reach. Watching the door the best he could to make sure that no one came too close to it.

His worry for Christina had him too distracted to pay attention to the fighting as much as he should have. Barely turning around in time to parry the sword that was coming at him, he got knocked down quickly. He continued to block swing after swing as he attempted to get off the floor. Before he could get all the way up James came running by and swung his sword, taking off the man's head.

Alex jumped to his feet, wiping the blood splatter off his face as he did.

He heard some fighting going on in the captain's cabin, but he knew it was just Christina trying to get out of her confinement. He ignored it and focused on dodging the sword that was coming towards his face. He ducked under it and quickly came back up as he retaliated the man's swing, his sword slid across the man's side, but not before the man's sword gouged into his thigh. He groaned but was thankful when the man fell to the ground, stopping the sword from going any deeper into his leg.

Attempting to continue in the battle he started to limp towards another intruder but before he could reach his target someone came from beside him and sucker-punched him. He felt the sting of the hit, but that was it.

PART 3

A CAPTIVE'S LIFE

CHAPTER 16

Christina hurried to get dressed, as soon as she dressed she headed to grab her weapons but the second she did the door to the captain's cabin slammed shut. She grabbed her sword and ran towards the door, but she was locked in. Angrily, she started pounding her fists on the door, screaming at them to let her out. Growing more furious with every failed attempt she began to kick and even swing her sword at the door, even though she knew she would never cut through it.

She tossed her sword on the bed and continued to wiggle the doorknob, hearing the clinking and clanking of swordfights outside the door, she knew that they meant to lock her in there. She was furious and she would make sure they all knew it when they let her out. Thinking of the punishment she would give the crew she heard a loud thud and turned quickly to see someone had come in through the porthole.

Reaching for her sword, but not being as fast as he was, she was left defenseless. She fought the best she could but before she knew it he had a hold of her and held some cloth over her nose. The smell of it was strong, and first came a slight headache, then everything went black.

When she awoke she was locked in a brig of some sort, but it wasn't on her own ship. The wood was a darker color than the wood on her ship and the cells were smaller. There was a blanket folded nicely with a pillow laid on top of it in one of the corners of the cell.

As her eyesight started to adjust, she could still feel the headache from earlier, but she also heard footsteps coming down the stairs. She stood quickly to see her captor. He had salt and pepper colored hair. He was slim but tall. His hair was short and for some reason he reminded her of Alex.

"Who the hell are you?" She demanded as he got next to the cell she was locked in.

"I am Alejandro Boseuilla." He stated, with the same kind smile Alex had.

"You are Alex's father." She stated, surprised, but not as surprised as she should have been.

"Alexander, yes, and I have been watching you two, fighting constantly, it seems the only time you two get along is when your being intimate." He answered bluntly.

"That's not true." Christina yelled. "I love him."

"If you loved him dear, do you really think you would hurt him so badly?" He questioned.

She hung her head in shame. "I don't try to." She answered.

"Then why do you do it?" He questioned. "You're obviously not right for him. He deserves to marry a rich woman, not a simple servant that ran away after murdering her master."

"I was defending myself, and I am rich now." She spat back.

"It don't matter dear, you were born poor, you'll find yourself poor again, and I will be damned if you use my son to keep money coming in." Alejandro returned.

"I'm not using him for anything." Her rage was apparent as she slammed the palms of her hands against the bars of the cell.

"You used him to mutiny against your old captain, so you could be captain of the ship. You used him as a safety net, which you are still doing." Alejandro coldly answered.

"That was his idea." She stated. "I never wanted to be captain, I took the position for him."

"That might be what you told yourself dear, but I know you would have done anything so you didn't have to worry about getting caught and marooned, if they didn't turn you in, you see, I know that there is a hefty bounty on your head right now."

"You're not going to turn me in are you?" She plead.

"No, you are more useful to me alive, I have a chance of getting my son back without having to injure him. I'm not sure if I am going to have you break his heart, or completely destroy him."

"I'd never do that to Alex." She interrupted.

"Then I'll just have to hold you captive until he comes to bargain for you." Alejandro answered.

Before she could even attempt to talk to him another man came down the stairs and grabbed her arm through the bars, shoving a cloth in her face. She remembered the smell instantly but as she tried to fight it, it got worse and everything went black again.

When she awoke again she was in a bedroom with a neatly made bed, the windows were barred so she couldn't get out. She figured she would try the door, but as she suspected the door was locked from the outside. She kicked at the door several times, trying to get out, but there wasn't even a sound of cracking, or the door getting ready to fall off the hinges. Before she could finish kicking at the door and trying to get out there was a knock, so she backed away wondering if she would be able to get out of the room.

At first it was just a young woman that walked in, she remembered the way she dressed all too clearly, she was obviously one of the Boseuilla servants, but she was accompanied by two men carrying flintlock pistols. She carried a huge bucket of water and started filling a tub up.

"What's going on?" Christina asked.

"Mr. Boseuilla requested that you get washed up for dinner." The servant woman stated, her voice was kind but you could plainly hear exhaustion in sounding in her voice.

"I don't want to join him for dinner." Christina returned.

"He knew you would say that, but he said if you don't come to dinner tonight you will be locked in the room when Alexander gets here." The servant answered.

"What does it matter if I get to see Alex or not?" She questioned.

"I don't know, he didn't expect you to argue that one." The servant returned.

"Do the guards have to be here when I bathe?" She questioned.

"No, they will wait outside of the door, with it locked." The servant answered. "I am required to bathe you though."

"Fine." She surrendered, outside of seeing Alex again, she didn't care, but Mr. Boseuilla knew that already.

The guards walked out the door then, she heard them lock it as soon as they shut it. The servant woman helped her undress and bathe. Then she went to the closet and grabbed a nice dress for her to wear. Christina was surprised that there were dresses in the room, it looked like it hadn't been lived in at all until she got there. She was reluctant on walking out of the room dressed as she was, she had never worn clothing like that before and she felt really uncomfortable. However she went anyways.

She looked around as they led her down to the dining room. Trying to remember the layout of where she was located in the overly large house. When they got to the dining room she sat down quietly, not wanting to do anything to make Mr. Boseuilla mad. She was worried about what he would do to Alex if she did something to make him mad. She thought about making a run for it, but there were too many guards and she had no weapons.

Mr. Boseuilla walked in then, a beautiful older woman was on his arm. She had high cheekbones and dark lips. Her skin tone was a little darker than Alex's and Mr. Boseuilla's. "Christina, this is my wife Anna." He said.

As Christina watched Mr. Boseuilla pull out a chair for his wife, she noticed there was no emotion in his eyes toward the woman, and she had none for him either as she thanked him. She could plainly see what Alex was running from, but from what Mr. Boseuilla was saying to her earlier she started to doubt her relationship with Alex as well. She thought she loved him, but if they did marry, would they live a loveless life like his parents?

"So my dear, you have seen part of my house, part of my fortune, the empire I have built for my son to one day take over. Tell me, what you have to offer him that is more than he already has." Alejandro started. "You have no home, no fortune that is truly yours, no family, and no empire."

"I have plenty to offer him." She barked back.

His laugh was as cold as his stare. "And what is that? Stolen goods and a big boat?"

"My ship is my home, my goods are my fortune, and the ocean is my nation. My crew is my family and to top it all off, I have his love, the love of my crew and the respect of any who dare cross us." She returned calmly as her food was set in front of her.

Mr. Boseuilla's facial expression turned to one of shock. She had never felt better in her life as she stood up to continue her explanation of her life. "My reign over the seas was brought by what I have proven I could do, not the money I have, I earned my respect, and I wasn't born into it. I have a life that was earned, not given, your 'empire' will fall as soon as your family runs out of money, mine will never because I have earned the respect of just about everyone that sails the same seas as I do. So you tell me how your life is better than mine?" Her words came out fierce.

Mr. Boseuilla stammered then sat quiet for the rest of the meal. She knew that wasn't going to be the last time she had to stand up for herself like that, but it felt amazing when she did. She always thought of herself as a pirate, nothing more. But the words that flowed out of her mouth couldn't be truer. She was a queen of the high seas, and she worked hard to make it that way. None of the pirates that had faced her, dared face her again, and always trusted her if they needed assistance.

She ate her meal, thanked the Boseuillas, and simply returned to her confinement. She was pleased with herself for the first time in a long time, and she wished that Alex was there to see how strong she had been. The thought of Alex just made her sad again though. She missed him more than she ever thought possible. She hoped he had come up with a plan to save her.

CHAPTER 17

Alex awoke with a splitting headache. He sat up, looking around the ship, pleased to see that no one was seriously injured. Tyler knelt down next to him. "How are you feeling Alex?" He asked.

"Other than my head hurting I feel fine." Alex answered. "Where's Christina?" He said as he jumped to his feet quickly.

"I don't know, she disappeared sometime during the fight." Tyler answered. "I think you were right, we checked the entire ship and she is nowhere on board."

"We had her locked in the captain's cabin, how the hell did someone get in there and out with her without being seen?" He questioned furiously. He started pacing the ship back and forth frantically. He turned and looked at all the people there just standing and watching him. "For heaven's sake find my wife." He demanded, quickly to correct himself though. "My fiancé."

"Calm down Alex, we're on the ships tail, maybe a day or two behind them." Oliver said. "We won't let them take our Captain from us. Go get yerself a drink lad, ye need it."

Before he could even turn to go down to the barracks, Tyler was shoving a cup of rum at him.

"We will find her, no matter what it takes Alex, but I am sure you already know where she might be." Tyler assured.

"You're right, I do know exactly where she is, and I will kill my father for this. I know what he's up to, and it will not work. Set sail for Vera Cruz, take the quickest route." He demanded as he quickly tossed back his mug of rum. "James, sharpen every sword aboard this ship, and Oliver take count of all the gun powder. I will blow their ship to smithereens before they even know that we are headed to Vera Cruz."

"Aye Captain." They answered.

He hated being called that, even though he and Christina were both technically the captains he didn't want anything to do with the name. He shook it off though and started working on getting all the sails down. He tried to keep himself busy just to keep his mind off of Christina but he wasn't really able too. Every time he turned around he could have sworn he heard her barking orders at the crew as she usually did.

He was worried sick at what could be happening to Christina. He knew his father would use her as leverage to bring him home, but he wasn't sure what he would do to her in the meantime. For all he knew his father could have her chained up and be torturing her or starving her, or even worse, he could be trying to convince her to leave him.

The days were unbearable even the weather was wonderful, and his nights were long and lonely. He found it impossible to sleep without Christina there. He eventually just stopped trying to sleep and stayed out on deck, staring through Henry's spyglass to see how close they were getting to Vera Cruz. Tyler walked out on deck startling him shortly after.

"Are you alright Alex?" Tyler asked.

"We're almost there, we should be there tomorrow." Alex returned ignoring the question.

"I know, but you have barely slept, mate. How are we supposed to come up with a plan to get Christina back if you haven't slept?" Tyler returned.

"He's right captain." An unusual voice stated.

Alex looked towards the stairs to the barracks where the voice had come from. It wasn't until she walked out from the shadows that they realized it was Zendaya speaking. She normally didn't speak to any of the men aboard and rarely spoke to the women.

"How are you supposed to have energy to rescue someone if you haven't been able to get any rest?" She asked.

"I can't stand to lay in that bed without her." Alex shook his head as he answered.

"You don't eat, you don't drink, and you can't sleep. Your mind is clouded by your loss. If you insist on embarking on this adventure, treat it like it's not the woman you love that was taken, but just an ordinary member of the crew." Zendaya's wise words sunk into his head. "What would you do if it was someone else?"

Alex thought about it, long and hard, but Tyler and Zendaya both stood there waiting for an answer. "I would send James and Tyler to go rescue her while I sat down with my father to talk. I would have them sneak into the house and get her safely out."

"Now considering that it is Christina what do you want to do?" Zendaya asked.

"I want to charge in there and kill everyone that stands in my way." Alex answered.

"I think for the safety of Christina that you should do what you would for anybody else. Love is an emotion that can bring out so many other emotions that it can be catastrophic." She said as she started to walk back to the barracks. "Good night." She added as she winked at Tyler.

"I think that is the first time I have ever heard her speak." Alex stated.

"She's very quiet, but very wise." Tyler returned.

"How did she know you were coming up here?" Alex asked.

Tyler scratched the back of his head and he shied away from the answer. "We should be to Vera Cruz early so you do need to get some rest, or at least try."

"Tyler, you can tell me you don't have to hide it unless she's unwilling nothing is going to happen to you."

"She's willing." Tyler returned. "You should know better than to have to ask me that."

"I didn't really think she was interested in anyone aboard the ship." Alex answered.

"That's because nobody talks to her, and she doesn't talk to anyone, but me." Tyler stated. "She's really sweet and very wise for her age."

"Well I'm happy that she makes you happy, but how could you not tell me?" Alex asked.

"It didn't really happen until after Christina was gone, before that we were just friends and it just kind of happened. She came into my room wanting to talk and it just happened." Tyler answered. "You were upset so I didn't say anything."

"So you and James be ready to go first thing in the morning when we make port, I'll give you a map with the back ways to my father's house, then we will get Christina back." He said. "I want you and James to plan how you are going to get her out, because like Zendaya said, I'm not thinking very clearly."

Tyler nodded his agreement. "Go get some sleep mate, or at least try to." Tyler said and patted Alex on the back. He turned and walked down to the barracks.

Alex took one more long look through the spyglass then just went into the captain's cabin. He took one of the maps Henry had drawn up and marked the pathway for James and Tyler. As soon as he was done he laid down on the bed, rubbing his hand on the part where Christina used to lay. Without even realizing it his fingers traced the outline of her body and his eyes started to water. He pulled her pillow into the spot that she use to lay and just put his arm over it like he used to. He closed his eyes, forcing them to stay shut, knowing that he wouldn't sleep he at least wanted to feel like it.

CHAPTER 18

Christina had spent a couple of days locked away in the room. She had barely gotten to speak to anyone besides the servant that had been tending to her. She was fed three times a day, and she was fed like royalty but she was still captive in the room that she had woken up in. She felt so alone without Alex, even with the friendship she had formed with the servant Tabitha that had been taking care of her every need. She rolled over in the bed and then heard the light knock that she had gotten used to.

Tabitha walked in the room then. "Good morning miss." She said as she locked the door behind her. She carried Christina's tray of food to the bed and set it down in front of Christina.

"Thank you Tabitha." Christina answered.

"You're welcome miss" Tabitha returned. "I have some wonderful news for you."

Christina sat up. Tabitha and her had made an agreement her second day there that if Christina got rescued she would try to take Tabitha with her, and Tabitha would keep her updated on what was going on.

"Alexander was spotted on the harbor and his father sent out some men to go search him out today. I sent a letter with a close friend of mine to tell him what room you are in, if he denies his father after seeing you they will just bring you back up here and they will be able to get you out." Tabitha said.

"What about you?" Christina asked.

"Around supper time they have me make all the beds and I always make this one last so that we can talk after supper. I figure I'll just take a little longer in here." Tabitha answered. "If something goes wrong with the plan I have sent to Alexander though, I want you to go, without me if you have to."

"Tabitha we made a deal." Christina whispered. "I'm not going without you."

"Please, because if Alexander does not take his father's deal, they plan to kill you after a week's time, and I do not want to see my only friend killed."

"But if they find out that you had anything to do with this they will kill you instead." Christina returned.

"They will never know that I had anything to do with your escape." She answered. "I have cut through the bars on the window and I will take the bars out when you go to supper so that they see that they will be able to get up here. I have rope in your closet ready for you."

"Thank you again Tabitha, you have been such a good friend to me." Christina said.

"As you have been to me miss." Tabitha returned. "Now eat up, you are going to need your strength for when Alexander comes to save you. Then we need to get you in a bath and all dressed up like Master Boseuilla wants."

Christina hurriedly scarfed down her food, anxiously waiting for supper time to come. She knew with Alex there that Mr. Boseuilla would want her downstairs to eat, which seemed to be what Tabitha's plan was running on. However she would just have to wait and see what was going to happen.

*****

Alex was startled to a banging on his door. He hadn't fallen asleep but he wasn't ready to leave the comfort of his memories. He tried to ignore the banging but it just continued until he got up and answered it. He crankily stared at Tyler.

"First we are at port, second, I have received a letter that you should look at, from the Boseuilla house." Tyler said.

He took the folded piece of parchment out of Tyler's hand and read the words, written so sophisticatedly that he knew it was written by his father. He was familiar with the handwriting from when his father would write down the inventory aboard his merchant ships. He focused on the words on the parchment.

Alexander, I have Christina locked away we can discuss what I want for her freedom. Come to the house around supper time, which is the same time as always. If you don't come she will suffer a fate worse than death.

Alejandro Boseuilla

"Flip it over." Tyler said.

Alex did and saw a different handwritten letter on the back of it.

Ms. Christina is held on the right side of the house, second story in the second bedroom, which is the third window on that side. I have cut out the bars to window and put them back in place so it looks like nothing has happened. If you send one or two people to sneak around to that side to come here to get her you won't have to do what Mr. Boseuilla wants. I just ask that when he takes Ms. Christina to dinner you request that she be sent back up. You will act as a distraction while your companions get her out. Ms. Christina and I will get out of this house and join you in the life that you wish to live.

Tabitha

"Do you think it's a trap?" Tyler asked. He had been reading over Alex's shoulder.

"No, Tabitha has been a servant for my father for a long time, and I was entrusted in her care a lot of times. I know how badly she wants to get away from my father. She was about six or seven years old when she was brought to the house. She's only a couple of years older than me."

"What if it is though?" Tyler returned.

"That's why I am sending you and James, you two are the best with a sword aboard this ship besides me and Christina." Alex stated. "And I know that you two genuinely care about Christina."

"So does everyone else that has been aboard this ship from the start, but I guess you are right." Tyler answered.

"I drew up a map on how to get to the house from back roads, so you two won't get caught. You and James should start preparing." Alex said.

As soon as Tyler nodded his agreement Alex turned and walked into the captain's cabin. He felt excited knowing that he was so close to getting Christina back, but all the possibilities started running through his head. He worried that something would go wrong and she would already be dead, or that James and Tyler would get caught with her and all three of them would be murder. His heart started aching at the thought of losing Christina forever.

Time went by slowly as all the outcomes ran through his head, and it became hard to breathe when there was a knock at the captain's cabin door. "Time to go." James' voice came through the door. Alex got up and rushed to stick a knife in his boot enough that no one would see it. He knew his father would have someone search him for weapons.

He, Tyler, and James climbed into a rowboat and some of the other crew members lowered them down. Alex separated from the other two as soon as they got to the shore. He watched as Tyler and James slipped down an alley. He continued on the main road to his father's house, gory images of what could happen to Christina repeatedly rushed through his head, almost taking the breath from his chest. Then he came to the big solid oak doors. The house loomed over him as if it was from the worst of his dreams. He took a deep breath and knocked on the door.

It wasn't much of a surprise that Tabitha had to be the one to answer the door. Tabitha always answered the doors. She smiled kindly at him. "Mr. Alex, it is good to see you doing so well. I assume that everything is well." She drug out the word well, he knew what she meant.

"Yes everything is as I had hoped." He returned. "I assume my father will be down in ten or so minutes." He walked in the door further to allow her to close the door.

She nodded catching on to what he meant. "Your father is in the dining room awaiting your arrival." She said.

He nodded his head and walked through the dining room door. He hadn't forgotten the layout of the house, nor would he ever. All of his memories were there, up until when he left. Which included the good and the bad. As he looked around the dining room the first thing he spotted was Christina, sitting in a chair at the head of the table, with guards surrounding her.

Her father was seated at the side next to her and his mother was on the other side, leaving him a spot across the table from her.

"Christina are you alright?" He asked, rushing to her side only to be stopped by one of the guards.

"I am fine Alex." She answered.

Alex backed away from her and sat at the spot left for him at the table. His father turned his attention to Alex then. "Tell me son how was your journey here?" Alejandro asked.

"Honestly it was terrible." Alex snapped at the man that always tried to ruin his life. Alejandro's fingers started tapping on the table.

"I am sure you are hungry." Alejandro said as he signaled for the cook to bring in the food.

Seconds later a plate was being set down in front of all of them except for Christina. Alex was instantly insulted that they didn't set down a plate for Christina, but then the guards walked over to her and forced her out of the chair. "I don't want to go yet." She yelled.

"Too bad dear." Alejandro answered.

She started struggling with the guards and screaming. "Alex whatever they want you to do don't do it." She yelled. "I love you."

Alex got up to rush towards her but he got himself under control and sat down knowing that she would be freed and he would be able to be with her again. "I can't believe that you would take the woman I love from me and treat her like a prisoner." Alex said with his teeth clenched so hard he thought they would chip.

"Sit down boy, she has been treated well. Eat some food, hers is up in her room." Alejandro answered. "Eat so we can discuss the harlot you have chosen to marry."

"She's no harlot." Alex returned.

"Eat, boy."

"I'm not hungry, let's discuss Christina, what do you want from me?" He asked.

"I want you to come home, no more of this pirate nonsense."

"Never."

"I'll kill her." Alejandro returned, the cold stare in his eyes showing just how little he cared about Christina.

"And if I do decide to stay?" Alex questioned.

"I will let her go back to her unruly life as a pirate. And you will wed whoever I tell you to or I will find her again and take her down with that mangy group of people that you call a crew." He sipped from his glass of wine and set it back down on the table. "I'll give you a week to think about it." Alejandro answered. "As for now I have business to attend to." He got up from the table and walked away, signaling one of the guards that accompanied Christina up to the room, to escort Alex out of the house.

Alex went with the guard with no argument. He held back his smile knowing that his father had given them a week to get away. His excitement overwhelmed him as the solid oak doors got shut behind him.

*****

Christina was almost in tears as the guards pulled her back up to her room, they didn't even give her a chance to kiss him. She missed him so much and they just drug her away like she didn't have a place there. She knew she didn't have any business to be down there but she had every right to be with Alex. The tears started flowing down her face as the guards shut her door and locked it behind them. She wiped her tears and tried to control her sobbing. Then two very familiar faces came out of her closet followed by Tabitha.

"Tyler, James." She said out of shock. She looked around to see that the bars had been taken out of the window.

She smiled big as Tabitha tied a rope to the bed and they hurriedly started to climb down it. She was anxious to get away, glad to see that her crew cared enough to come after her. As soon as her feet touched the ground she started running towards the harbor. The dress she was forced to wear made it difficult so she tore it up until it was easier to run in and continued on until she reached the ship.

Christina glanced around the ship, searching for Alex but he didn't seem to be aboard the ship yet. Starting to panic and think that something went wrong she continuously searched the ship for him until she came up from the barracks and saw him boarding. She took a deep breath and ran to him, jumping in his arms. He squeezed her tightly as he lifted her up. He kissed her lips roughly, just as glad to see her free as she was to be free.

He looked at the crew that was just standing around. “Get this ship back on the water, we don’t have much time to lose my father, we need to get out of sight as quickly as possible. Make way to Tortuga so we can get a new ship, we need to throw them off track.” He demanded.

The crew started working but he carried Christina into the captain’s cabin. Closing the door with his foot, he unlaced the dress she was wearing then laid her on the bed. Slowly pulling her dress off he kissed his way down her body until she was bare. Kissing his way back up her body he took her nipple into his mouth and started lightly sucking on it, letting his tongue swirl around it. He spread her pussy lips with one hand as he lightly ran his finger on her clit.

Hearing her moaning and groaning he switched over to the other nipple and slid his finger inside her. He wanted so badly to put his dick in her, but he wanted to hear her cum first. Knowing he wouldn’t be able to last long he continued thrusting his finger in and out of her, also rubbing her clit with his thumb. Her moaning got louder as she started to push herself towards him. He could feel his finger get wetter as her pussy walls started to convulse. He pulled his finger out and pulled his trousers down. Pushing his hardened shaft into her, he could feel that she was still orgasming and continued rubbing her clit with his thumb as he slowly pushed his cock into her, then slowly pulled out to where only the head was still inside. Her moaning turned into screaming so Alex grabbed a pillow and put it over her mouth as he started thrusting in and out, harder and faster.

He could feel himself getting close, and the more she screamed the worse it got. He tried to keep it from happening as long as he could until he finally exploded. Collapsing on the bed next to her he ran his fingertips down her abdomen, barely even touching her. He kissed her lips vigorously. "I'll be back luv, and I'll make you scream like that again." He said as he got off the bed and pulled his trousers back on.

She still hadn't caught her breath, so she didn't get to argue before he walked out of the door. He walked out to see that the ship was a ways away from port, but not as far as he would like it to be. Tyler walked up to him then.

"The rest of the crew went to bed, I put Tabitha in the room with Zendaya. I told her we can get to the articles in the morning." Tyler said.

"You're on night watch tonight?" Alex asked.

"Yes." Tyler answered.

"So mine is tomorrow then." Alex stated.

"Yes." Tyler returned. "But I'm sure you can get someone else to do it."

"No, just cause I got Christina back doesn't mean that I am going to force someone else to take my night shift, I'll just make her stay up with me." Alex returned.

Alex walked down to the barracks and grabbed himself and Tyler a cup of rum. As soon as he handed the extra cup to Tyler he downed his glass, making a sour face at the end of it. He bid Tyler goodnight and walked back into the captain's cabin to see Christina curled up underneath the blanket. He got under the blanket with her and pulled her close against him. He kissed her jawline as he circled his finger around her bare stomach.

He tried to stay awake and just enjoy her being there but he succumbed to sleep quickly, finally able to sleep easily.

CHAPTER 19

The voyage to Tortuga didn't take much time, and with Christina back, things felt normal aboard the ship again. However, finding a ship to trade was deemed nearly impossible, and no one wanted to leave the ship in the hands of another. After looking at almost every ship that people were willing trade, none of them were good enough. After searching for what felt like endless hours Pete and Xavier decided to just remodel the ship and paint the outside of it so that it looked different than it was. Unfortunately, with the entire crew working on it, it would still take a couple of days.

They all worked as late as possible and were up as early as possible in the mornings. By the time it was all done it had been a week already. Alex knew then that his father would have one of his ships out looking for him and Christina. They finished the ship late at night and the crew members were all exhausted, even all the women aboard helped as much as they possibly could. They all wanted to get to bed, but Alex demanded that they all got on the ship and got it moving. Once the ship was good and on the water, Alex allowed all the crew members to go to sleep, he volunteered to be on the night watch that night just so that the rest of the crew would get the rest needed.

His night went by slowly, and very uneventful, but once the crew started waking up he headed into the captain's cabin to rest up as much as he possibly could, but even with Christina back, sleeping was nearly impossible without her in the room with him. He laid there waiting to just fall asleep, but before he could Christina walked through the door.

"What do you need, Luv?" He asked.

"I just needed my hat, it's a hot day." She answered. "I thought you would be asleep by now."

"After you were taken I found it rather difficult to sleep without you in the bed next to me." He returned.

She smiled sweetly and walked over to the bed. She pulled the covers up and slid in next to him. He pulled her against him, wrapping his arms around her tightly, as if he didn't she'd get taken again. Without fail, ten minutes later he was seeing the insides of his eyelids.

Christina waited until she could hear his breathing slow, but when it did, she felt no urge to leave his arms. She missed him just as much as he missed her, if not more. She loved feeling his warmth wrapped around her again. She laid there, until she was sure that she would fall asleep too if she stayed any longer. She forced herself to get out of bed, she grabbed her tricornered hat and walked out of the room quietly.

As she walked out of the captain's cabin, she saw one of the Boseuilla ships passing by them, hoping that they didn't notice her. Tyler ran up to her then. "I think we need to worry about finding a place to hide for a while." He said, his eyes wide.

"Did they recognize any one of us?" She questioned.

"They came awfully close to the ship for comfort." He stated. "I bet they are planning as we speak."

"Tell Henry to head to the island where we found the 'Forbidden Plunder'." She started. "We will hide in the caves if we have too. There is food and decent water there we could stay there for months." She added.

"Aye, Captain." Tyler returned as he quickly walked down the stairs to the barracks. He was gone maybe a few minutes before he walked back up. "Should I inform Alex?"

"No, he just fell asleep, I will inform him when he wakes." She answered. "Meanwhile, make sure that all the pistols are on someone's hip, loaded at all times until we know we are safe. I want everyone to have their weapons on them, or at least easily accessible at all times." She said loudly, so that the crew members on deck could hear her.

Person after person went and grabbed their weapons, strapping them to their bodies so that they would be easy to get to if needed. They all stood at the ready, watching what the ship was doing, however Christina was sure that they wouldn't let it be noticeable as to what they were going to do.

She kept watching the ship, nervously, her hands were shaking. She knew what would happen to her this time, and she was terrified. They warned her that if she were to get out, they would kill Alex in front of her. She had no clue how a father could be willing to kill their own child, but she could tell that Alejandro meant it. She didn't dare find out how bad life would be without Alex in it. She felt tears starting to form in her eyes at the thought of it. She turned and walked down to the barracks to try and compose herself better. She wiped the tears and turned to go back upstairs but was startled by Alex standing behind her.

"What's wrong, me amore?" He asked sweetly as he wrapped his arms around her shoulders, pulling her head into his chest.

"We passed by one of your father's ships, I am pretty sure they recognized us." She answered.

"They probably didn't Christina." He returned.

"They came really close to the ship, and I walked out of the captain's cabin. I saw the same man that kidnapped me, and I know he saw me too." She stated.

"We will just find somewhere to hide." Alex reassured her.

"I told Henry to take us to where we found the treasure and we can just all hide on the island, we can all fit in the cave where we found the treasure and be comfortable for a while." She answered.

"Ok, then that is the plan." He kissed her forehead lovingly. "They won't get their hands on you again."

"That's not what I'm worried about." She returned. "Your father said if I escaped, he'd kill you."

"He can try, but he won't succeed." Alex answered. "Everything will be fine."

Christina smiled and stood on her toes to kiss his lips. She walked back on deck, and just waited for night to come. She couldn't wait to get to the hidden island so they could be safe. But the time went by slowly, it drug on and on, and it seemed that they passed through more storms than ever before. As the storms got worse, Alex didn't fret. He knew that once they reached the hidden island that they would know freedom. Then from there they could make it look like the ship wrecked and they all died. Then he and Christina could hopefully live their lives the way they wished.

Upon reaching the hidden island Alex started telling the crew the plan. "Once we reach the island, Henry will get us as close to shore as possible, from there we will need to tie a few lines to the main mast so we can pull the ship up on land so we can hide it in the trees. We are going to need everybody's help. All hands on deck. We will get everything prepared to take off the ship now so we can start when we get to land. By taking all the heavy stuff off the ship it will make it easier to move. Then we will drag over the ship that wrecked here a while ago so it looks knew, and we will drag the skeletons over to the water to make it seem like we all died." He knew his plan was nearly perfect. "Get to work." Was the last demand he had?

Henry was the first to move, and he headed straight down to his chart room. The rest of the crew started shuffling down to the barracks and doing as they were told, two or more of them moving one cannon up the stairs at a time.

It took them all day to get the ship hidden, and the tallest trees barely hid the main mast, once they checked that the ship was hidden well enough for intruders not to be suspicious they started moving all the stuff they had taken off the ship. By the time they were finished they were all exhausted to the point that they could sleep anywhere that they could lay their heads. Heading back to the ship they all drug their feet and went straight to bed.

As soon as the sun peaked through the port holes they all awoke. Some had to be shaken to wake but most of them didn't. Henry instantly went out with his spy glass to the edge of the trees. Looking out over the horizon could see what looked like the top of the main mast of the ship that had been hunting them. Unsure he looked closely, then decided it was best to go warn Alex and Christina so he rushed back to the hidden ship.

"Captain, I do believe that ship is headed here, we have maybe a few hours before they can see what we are doing." He warned.

Christina and Alex both froze, uncertain about what they should do, but Oliver stepped up quickly to give the new demands. "Alex and Christina will go hide in the hidden cave where we found all the skeletons and treasure, all the women will go with them. We will instead of moving the ship wreck where we planned, we will tear it up more and drag it a little ways towards where we came in. We only have a few hours but since it's rotted and torn to shreds it shouldn't weigh as much, meanwhile the ones hiding will get the skeletons and stuff outside of the cave for easier and quicker access for us. Henry we keep watch." Oliver demanded. "Go now!"

All of them started rushing off the ship and got to work on what they were told to do. Christina and Alex hurried to show the women where the cave was, considering that none of them were there the first time they were there. Christina rushed them in through the waterfall and urged all of them to drag a body out as soon as they came across one. Alex took the bones and skeletons and stacked them all up so that no one had to come through the water. Once that was done they rushed through the now clean tunnel and to the hollowed out cave.

They anxiously waited for the rest of the crew to get back, it took them all about an hour to start shuffling into the cave. They kept quiet, unsure of if the other ship's crew would explore the island. They waited until it started to get dark, then Henry snuck out with his spyglass in hand to check and see if they could see the ship anywhere. He was pleased to see that they were nowhere in sight and signaled the rest of them that everything was alright.

They spent almost a week on the island, checking the ship for any damages that could have happened while they drug it on the land, and making any repairs that seemed necessary. Once the repairs were done they got the ship back on the water and prepared to leave. Most of the crew went to bed as soon as dinner was done. Tyler, Oliver, Christina, and Alex were the only ones left out on deck.

"So what are we going to do when we leave here?" Tyler asked.

"I'm not sure, I thought of taking cover in Port Royal for a while." Christina answered.

"What if we go to Barbados?" Alex returned.

"I can't go to Barbados, what if I am found out?" Christina stated.

"What if you were kidnapped, by pirates and were rescued?" Alex asked.

"I suppose that could work, or we could go to the other end of the island, but I am not sure if I am comfortable with that." Christina said.

"What about Puerto Rico, or maybe Tortuga." Tyler suggested.

"Would Tortuga be a good place to raise a child?" Christina asked as she lightly rubbed her stomach.

"Are you serious?" Alex asked, eyes wide as a smile spread across his lips.

"I think so." Christina answered.

"Well that depends on if you want your child to be a pirate." Tyler returned.

"What do you want Alex?" Christina asked.

"If we go to Tortuga, we will still be able to see our crew, and we can build our house away from the town so that the baby isn't exposed to most the stuff that goes on there, plus we will be able to find them, and see if everything has died down so we can return, if we feel like it." Alex stated.

"So Tortuga it is." Christina answered. "I'll tell Henry in the morning."

EPILOGUE

The crew helped Christina and Alex build their house and buy the property they wanted. The crew voted Tyler to be the captain until Christina and Alex were ready to return, but after the birth of their child, they never did, although once their child, Tyler James, got older they told him all the stories they had of piracy. Though they never returned to piracy, it still held a place in their hearts, and the crew continued to visit as if they were still working together.

OTHER BOOKS

BY JESSICA KILLABREW

Forbidden Plunder

Stealing A Pirate's Heart
(Stealing A Pirate's Heart Book 1)
Mutiny of the Heart
(Stealing A Pirate's Heart Book 2)
Bounty of Her Heart
(Stealing A Pirate's Heart Book 3)

www.ingramcontent.com/pod-product-compliance
Lightning Source LLC
Chambersburg PA
CBHW072227190626
46809CB00017B/1308
9781945012389